ANNA-MAGDALENA
THE LITTLE GIRL WITH
THE BIG NAME

Page 3

ANNA-MAGDALENA
GOES HEAD OVER
HEELS

Page 95

KAY KINNEAR

Copyright © 1992, 1994, 1997 Kay Kinnear
This omnibus edition copyright © 1997 Lion Publishing

Published by
Lion Publishing plc
Sandy Lane West, Oxford, England
ISBN 0 7459 3756 X
Albatross Books Pty Ltd
PO Box 320, Sutherland, NSW 2232, Australia
ISBN 0 7324 1624 8

First edition of *Anna-Magdalena: The Little Girl with the Big Name* in 1992
First edition of *Anna-Magdalena Goes Head Over Heels* in 1994
This omnibus edition first published 1997
10 9 8 7 6 5 4 3 2 1 0

A catalogue record for this book is available
from the British Library

Printed and bound in Great Britain
by Cox & Wyman, Reading

ANNA-MAGDALENA:
THE LITTLE GIRL WITH THE BIG NAME

To Katie Kinnear
For all her help and advice

Anna-Magdalena: the little girl with the big name

Kay Kinnear

Illustrations by
Maureen Bradley

Contents

1

Anna-Magdalena is a Pest

Anna-Magdalena was a small person with a large name. She had blue eyes and orange hair with a straight fringe that she blew off her forehead whenever she was worried or cross. More times than not, her face wore a determined 'I-know-what-I-know' expression.

This morning what Anna-Magdalena knew was that her mum was busy. Anna-Magdalena was supposed to play quietly so that her mum could finish her work.

First she fed some fresh greens to Sam, her guinea-pig, and then she checked to see if he showed signs of growing a tail. Her mum said that guinea-pigs didn't have tails, but Anna-Magdalena was always hoping. A swishy black tail or a little white pompom would look so fetching on Sam's round bottom, that Anna-

Magdalena kept careful watch just in case.

Next, Anna-Magdalena rode her bike very fast on the path around the garden. Every day she tried to get all the way round before she counted to twenty. But as her pedalling got faster, her numbers speeded up too.

'Sixteen, seventeen, nineteen, twenty.'

Twenty already and she hadn't quite reached the shed.

Anna-Magdalena decided to try again later, but meanwhile she went to wave at Granny Charles who lived next door. Every morning Granny Charles sat at her window reading the Bible. It was a big book with lots of words and no pictures. Granny Charles had told Anna-Magdalena that it was full of stories about God and about Jesus.

'My day doesn't go right,' she'd once said to Anna-Magdalena, 'unless I start it by talking to my friend Jesus.'

Granny Charles always waved back when she saw Anna-Magdalena waving through the gap in the hedge. Sometimes if Granny was nearly finished with her reading, Anna-Magdalena was invited in for a glass of milk and a biscuit with chocolate bits in it. Of course, Granny Charles wasn't her real granny, but she was a real friend.

Granny often told her the story she had just been reading. Last week Anna-Magdalena had been surprised to hear how Jesus had made five loaves of bread and two small fish feed a whole crowd of hungry people.

Five thousand, Granny said. Anna-Magdalena wasn't too sure how many that was, but it sounded a lot.

There was another good thing about Granny Charles. She always called Anna-Magdalena by all of her name.

Her mum called her Mags. Her Uncle Andy mostly called her Mags. Her big friend Gerald, who was her mum's friend too, called her Mags. Her Aunty Cath called her Mags. And her Uncle Henry called her Sausage. But Granny Charles always called her Anna-Magdalena and that was nice.

Today, however, Granny Charles wasn't sitting at the window. Anna-Magdalena leaned through the gap in the hedge and tried to see if Granny Charles was in the back garden. The light was on in her kitchen, but Anna-Magdalena couldn't see her anywhere.

Anna-Magdalena went inside to tell her mum that Granny wasn't where she should be.

Her mum was still doing her work. There were some big, wide books with lines and numbers in them on the kitchen table.

'Mummy, Granny Charles isn't reading today.'

'Mmm,' her mum said, not looking up from her books. 'She'll probably be there in a minute. Go and look again.'

Anna-Magdalena returned to the gap in the hedge. Granny's comfortable chair was there all right, but Granny definitely wasn't.

'Granny Charles, Granny Charles—it's me, Anna-Magdalena,' she called. She waited but there was no answer.

She tried again, much louder this time.

'Granny Charles, Granny Charles—it's me, Anna-Magdalena!'

Still no answer. Anna-Magdalena went back into the kitchen.

'Mummy, Granny Charles *isn't* there. I called and called.'

'Mags, you are a pest. You know I've got to get Mr Rogers' accounts done now. Remember, I said if you kept busy this morning while I did my work, we'd make fairy cakes this afternoon and walk through the park to take the books to Mr Rogers.

'Go and play for a little while and then look again.'

Anna-Magdalena went outside and put her bear, who was called Bear, on the wall. Bear was going to count while she raced her bike round the garden.

'Fourteen, fifteen, seventeen, nineteen, twenty.'

This time she didn't even get near the shed. What's more, she had a suspicion that her counting wasn't perfect either.

It was hard to concentrate on pedalling a good race when she was thinking of something else.

She went back to the gap in the hedge to check on Granny Charles. Still not there. Anna-Magdalena was worried. She blew her fringe off her forehead and marched into the house.

Anna-Magdalena tugged at her mum's sleeve. 'She *isn't* there', she said.

Anna-Magdalena's mum sighed. Then she said, 'Mags, I've been thinking. Granny Charles has probably gone shopping.'

'Is today Wednesday?' Anna-Magdalena asked.

'Y-e-ss . . . '

'Granny always goes shopping on Tuesday when we go to the library. Please, Mummy, can we go and see?' And Anna-Magdalena hopped up and down and pulled her mum's arm.

Anna-Magdalena's mum sighed again and stood up. In the back garden Anna-Magdalena popped through the gap in the hedge while her mum who was too big to do that went round by the gate.

They knocked on the door.

They looked in at the window.

They went and called through the kitchen door. Then Anna-Magdalena's mum stood on tiptoe to look in at the high window.

'Oh no!' she cried.

'What, Mummy?'

'Granny has slipped and fallen. I think she was mopping the floor. Quick! Come with me.'

Anna-Magdalena and her mum raced back to their own house and phoned for an ambulance. Then her mum got out the key she kept for Granny's back door and they ran back to her house.

By the time the ambulance men arrived ten minutes later, Anna-Magdalena and her mum had covered Granny Charles with a blanket. Granny's eyes had started to flutter open.

Anna-Magdalena's mum talked to the men quietly as they lifted the old lady carefully onto the stretcher. The ambulance drove quickly away with the blue lights flashing.

'We must go and phone Granny's son so he can meet her at the hospital,' Anna-Magdalena's mum said.

That evening while Anna-Magdalena was eating her egg and toast soldiers the phone rang. Her mum talked for quite a long time and then came into the kitchen smiling.

'Mags, Granny Charles is going to be all right. She's had a nasty knock on the head and a broken wrist, but they think she can come home in a few days.'

'Granny's son says it was lucky we found her so soon after her fall. He thanked me for being such a good neighbour. I told him it was you who had pestered me into going to look for her.'

That night when Anna-Magdalena and her mum said their prayers together, Anna-Magdalena said, 'God bless Mummy. God bless Gerald. God bless

Uncle Andy. God bless Aunty Cath and Uncle Henry. God bless Granny Charles and make her well again.'

And Anna-Magdalena's mother said, 'God bless my good girl, Anna-Magdalena, who is the right kind of pest.'

Anna-Magdalena smiled with her eyes shut.

2
Anna-Magdalena
Has the Grumps

Anna-Magdalena had been out of sorts all day. Nothing pleased her. Whatever her mum suggested, Anna-Magdalena didn't want to do.

'No,' she said. 'No, I don't want to.'

Her mum suggested painting in the garden. She said, 'I'll clip a big sheet of paper with two clothes pegs onto your blackboard. And I'll mix up five lovely colours from the powder paints. Would you like to paint a picture for me?'

Anna-Magdalena blew the straight orange fringe off her forehead. She felt cross.

'No,' she said. 'No, I don't want to.'

'Well, all right,' said her mum and sighed. 'As soon as I've finished my work, we could make Smartie biscuits. You know, the ones you like so much.'

Anna-Magdalena usually loved cooking, especially

cakes and biscuits. These biscuits were special. With her mum's help, Anna-Magdalena knew how to stir together sugar and margarine. Then she knew how to add eggs and the flour.

Anna-Magdalena always did the last bit all by herself. She would open a packet of Smarties and drop the little round sweets into the bowl very slowly. She loved to stir the yellow, red, blue, green, pink, orange, brown and purple sweets into the mixture. Exactly three sweets were always allowed to find their way into her mouth. Altogether, making these biscuits was one of Anna-Magdalena's very favourite things.

So her mum was really surprised when Anna-Magdalena said, 'No, I don't want to. I don't want to make *anything*.'

Anna-Magdalena was a small, determined person, and today it was clear that she was determined to be miserable.

'Well, I give up,' said her mum, exasperated. 'Now you'll have to wait till Uncle Andy comes for you this afternoon. If he can't cheer you up, nobody can.'

This was true. Uncle Andy had the sunniest, smiliest face of anybody that Anna-Magdalena knew. It was nearly impossible to be in a bad temper when he was around.

Uncle Andy was her daddy's younger brother. Anna-Magdalena's daddy had died when she was just a baby, less than a year old. Her mum said he was in heaven with God now. Anna-Magdalena sometimes missed having a daddy and so she specially loved her Uncle Andy.

His hair was the same bright orange as Anna-Magdalena's. In summer, he got so many freckles that they almost joined up to make one giant all-over freckle. That's what Anna-Magdalena thought anyway.

After lunch, Uncle Andy breezed into the house. He didn't seem to notice Anna-Magdalena's grumpy face. He picked her up and whirled her around at great speed.

'How's my Maggy-Waggy today?' he cried, kissing her on the cheek.

Catching her breath and remembering that she was in a temper, Anna-Magdalena replied crossly, 'My name is Anna-Magdalena.'

'Why, so it is. I'll try to remember, Madame Anna-Magdalena,' Uncle Andy said, smiling.

Uncle Andy talked to her mum quietly. Then the little girl and her uncle went out of the door.

Her mum called after them, 'Mags, I don't want to see that grumpy face when you come back.'

Anna-Magdalena and Uncle Andy walked along in silence on the footpath towards the park.

After a time, he said, 'Do you know what *I* do when I'm in a bad mood and feeling full of the grumps?'

Anna-Magdalena stared up at him in great surprise.

Uncle Andy grinned at her startled face. 'Oh yes, me too. Everybody feels bad and out of sorts sometimes. But there are things you can do to help.'

Anna-Magdalena kicked a stone off the path and waited to hear what 'things' could possibly help.

'First,' said Uncle Andy, 'I send up a little prayer, just a short one. I say, "Please, dear Jesus, help me to get rid of my bad mood. Help me to be nicer to other people." '

'Oh,' said Anna-Magdalena. She thought about how she hadn't been very nice to her mum that morning.

'OK, Mags,' Uncle Andy said. 'Shall we say our little prayer together? Then I'll tell you what to do next.'

They said the little prayer and walked along quietly for a while. Then Uncle Andy added, 'God helps people who want to be helped. So next, let's try to think of three very nice things.'

He asked, 'Can you think of any nice things?'

Anna-Magdalena shook her head. At that moment, she really couldn't think of anything that was nice.

'All right,' said Uncle Andy. 'I'll think of some for you. Number One Nice Thing: you're going to spend the afternoon with me.'

Uncle Andy scooped up Anna-Magdalena again and whirled her around until she squeaked.

'I'm one of your favourite people, isn't that right?'

asked Uncle Andy, laughing.

Anna-Magdalena nodded. In spite of herself, a smile almost crept out around the corners of her mouth.

'I can't think of Number Two Nice Thing just now,' said Uncle Andy. 'So we'll go on to Number Three Nice Thing: I'm going to buy you an ice cream later.'

Anna-Magdalena loved ice cream, especially chocolate. So that *was* a nice thing.

'I know a nice thing,' said Anna-Magdalena, suddenly. 'You could take me on the high slide. I can't go on by myself.'

'Right you are,' said Uncle Andy. 'So we've got our Three Nice Things.'

The prayer and thinking of nice things made Anna-Magdalena feel a little bit better. She slipped her hand into Uncle Andy's as they walked along.

'Next,' continued Uncle Andy, 'to get rid of the grumps, we keep busy. We do whatever we do as well as we can so we haven't got time to be grumpy.'

They reached the park playground and at once tried out Uncle Andy's remedy.

They went down the longest, tallest slide at least a dozen times together. They whirled round and round on the roundabout until Uncle Andy staggered off saying he was dizzy. Anna-Magdalena crawled through a set of box shapes that her uncle was too big for. She hung upside down on the climbing frame.

They swung. They climbed. They jumped. They tried every single piece of play equipment in the park. Then they headed for the boating lake.

'We've played as well as we can. Now we're going to row very fast round the lake,' said Uncle Andy. 'Is my Anna-Banana a cheerful girl yet?'

'Well . . .' said Anna-Magdalena who didn't give up easily on anything, but the corners of her mouth twitched.

When they got to the lake, Uncle Andy dug into his pocket for some coins to hire a little bright green boat. He showed Anna-Magdalena how to sit in the middle of the boat facing the back. He called it the stern. They sat side by side, each with an oar.

At first they went round and round in a circle. Uncle Andy was so much bigger and stronger that every time he pulled on his oar, the boat went sideways. But when he began to help Anna-Magdalena when she pulled on her oar, they went through the water much better.

The lake was very shallow and they nearly got stuck on the bottom. But by pushing themselves free with an oar, splashing and laughing all the time, they finally made their way out to open water and eventually back to the hiring shed.

'We didn't row very fast, but did we do it as well as we could?' asked Uncle Andy.

'We did,' said Anna-Magdalena.

'And are you feeling really cheerful yet?' demanded Uncle Andy.

'Yes,' said Anna-Magdalena, and she gave her uncle a big grin.

'So, Mags, can you remember what to do for a bad mood next time?'

Anna-Magdalena thought. 'Say a little prayer to Jesus and ask him to help me.'

She thought some more. 'Think of Three Nice Things.'

She paused. 'And go rowing.'

Uncle Andy laughed delightedly. 'Well, do something—*anything*—with all your concentration and all your energy. It doesn't have to be rowing. Now let's go and get some ice cream.'

At the corner shop near the park, Uncle Andy read from the sign over the ice cream cabinet.

'There are Lemon Zoom Dooms. Whipped Whinges. Green Grumpies.' He glanced down to see if Anna-Magdalena realized he was making up ice creams.

He continued to pretend to read. 'Temper Tingles. Chocolate Whirly Twirly Swirlies. Moody Marvels.' Anna-Magdalena managed to keep a straight face and joined in Uncle Andy's game of silly ice creams.

She said, 'I'll have a Chocolate Whirly Twirly Swirly, please,' and giggled.

Uncle Andy laughed too. 'You knew all along I was

making them up. If I twirl you round twice and buy you a chocolate cornet, will that count as a Chocolate Whirly Twirly Swirly?'

'Yes,' said Anna-Magdalena, happily.

While she waited for her ice cream, Anna-Magdalena noticed a row of masks hanging up near some toys and games. There was a mask of a clown, an elf, a purple monster, and a frowning green man with a wart on his nose. She tugged at Uncle Andy's sleeve and he bent down to her level. Pointing at the frowning green man mask, she whispered something in her uncle's ear.

Twenty minutes later Uncle Andy and a short, frowning green man with a wart on his nose knocked on Anna-Magdalena's front door.

Anna-Magdalena's mum opened the door and jumped back in surprise.

Uncle Andy said solemnly, 'I believe you said you didn't want to see Anna-Magdalena's grumpy face when we came back, so we've brought you a different one. A different grumpy face.'

But something strange was happening to the short green man with a wart on his nose. Though he was still frowning, his body was giggling so much that he couldn't stand up and he had to sit down on the front step.

3

Anna-Magdalena
Makes a Friend

One Sunday morning Anna-Magdalena, a boy called Jack and four other children were sitting on a rug waiting for Sunday school to begin.

At Anna-Magdalena's church, Sunday school was held in the church hall. There were five little rooms, one for each group. Anna-Magdalena liked Sunday school because her teacher, Mrs Lander, was smiley and kind. Every week she told them interesting stories. Sometimes they were about Jesus and the good things he did. Sometimes they were about special people. Sometimes about ordinary people. There was always something to do after the story, and Anna-Magdalena liked that too.

'Jack, move over,' said Anna-Magdalena to the boy next to her on the rug. 'I haven't got enough room.'

Jack moved himself slowly to give Anna-Magdalena just a very tiny bit more space. Jack was a tall, strong, clever boy and he had firm opinions about things. Anna-Magdalena was a small, strong, clever girl and she also had firm opinions about things. Sometimes Jack and Anna-Magdalena got along well, but more often than not they argued.

Just then Mrs Lander came in with a new little boy. 'This is Neville,' she said. 'He's just moved from the country to live near our church.'

Mrs Lander asked Anna-Magdalena, Jack and the others in the class—Polly, Rajinder, Tommy and Kevin—to say their names one by one. The thin, silent little boy called Neville didn't look at the other children. He stared down at his feet.

'Can you make a place for Neville on the rug, please,' asked Mrs Lander. Nobody moved for a moment. Then Anna-Magdalena cheerfully bumped her small body against Jack and Polly to make space.

'There's room here for Neville,' she called. 'Come and sit here.' Without speaking, Neville folded himself into a small hunched shape beside Anna-Magdalena.

'Now,' said Mrs Lander, 'we'll have a story. Our story today is about people who lived a long, long time ago.'

Mrs Lander told the children about how those people took no notice of what God wanted, but did bad things instead. In the end God decided he would send a great flood of water to cover all the earth. But there was one good man God wanted to save—his name was Noah.

God told Noah to build a very large boat called an ark. Before the heavy rains came, Noah and his family and all kinds of animals and birds went into the ark. There were lions, tigers, elephants, giraffes—two of every creature living on earth. Then Noah loaded the ark with lots of food for the animals and people.

'How long were they in the boat?' asked Jack.

'It was a long time, just over a year,' said Mrs Lander.

But the story did have a happy ending. When Noah and his family were at last on dry land again, they thanked God for saving them. And God put a rainbow into the sky as a promise that he would never again let water cover the earth.

Anna-Magdalena and the others asked lots of questions about the story. But Neville, the new boy, didn't ask anything.

'Did you like the story, Neville?' asked Anna-Magdalena.

Neville slowly looked up from his feet and gave the very smallest of nods.

Mrs Lander clapped her hands and said, 'Now, we'll be doing Noah's ark pictures *next* week, but today we want to finish decorating our new folders!'

She turned to Neville. 'We're making folders to keep our pictures in till they're ready to take home.

What colour folder would *you* like to make, Neville?'

'Have blue,' urged Anna-Magdalena. '*Mine's* blue.'

Neville didn't say anything, but he gave the very smallest of nods.

The children went over to the work table and Anna-Magdalena chose a light blue folder for Neville. Then she found her own folder and looked at it carefully. It was pretty, she thought. The tree she had drawn on the folder was leaning a bit, but the bird was very good. It was as big as the tree. She took a crayon and began to colour the bird.

While she was colouring, she noticed Neville standing beside her holding his blue folder.

'Shall I help you, Neville?' asked Anna-Magdalena. Without waiting for an answer, she took the folder and pressed down the top flap. 'Now it's ready,' she said. 'You can do patterns on it. You can do fish. Or birds. Or trees. Or flowers. Or what do you like?'

Neville looked at Anna-Magdalena, but he didn't say anything.

Anna-Magdalena made a decision. 'Who's got the flower stencil?' she asked. Rajinder passed it down the table.

'Neville's having flowers,' said Anna-Magdalena, drawing three times round the flower stencil onto Neville's folder. 'There you are. All you've got to do is colour,' said Anna-Magdalena, handing Neville a crayon.

Mrs Lander asked Neville gently, 'Is that all right, Neville?'

He nodded the very smallest of nods and began to colour slowly.

'Don't you ever talk?' asked Jack.

'He doesn't have to,' said Anna-Magdalena, firmly defending her new friend.

'He probably can't get a word in edgeways with you two chatterboxes,' said Mrs Lander and she gave Neville a friendly pat on the shoulder.

After Sunday school Anna-Magdalena met her mum and their friend Gerald outside the church. She told them about the folders they'd been making and then all about Neville, her new friend.

'He doesn't talk,' said Anna-Magdalena. 'He doesn't do anything, so I help him. I helped him make his folder.'

'That's nice of you, Mags,' said her mum, 'but give him time to settle in.'

Gerald picked up Anna-Magdalena to give her a piggyback ride to his car. He said to her, 'One day, maybe Neville will surprise you.'

A week later, on the next Sunday morning, Anna-Magdalena met Neville going into the church hall.

'H'lo, Neville, you can sit by me today,' she said, smiling.

Neville gave the very smallest of nods.

When Mrs Lander arrived they talked about the story of Noah and the ark. Every child could remember something—about the rain, the boat, the food, the animals or the rainbow. Jack and Anna-Magdalena, of course, could remember lots of things.

Then Mrs Lander asked Neville, 'Do you remember the story, Neville?'

Neville gave the very smallest of nods, but he didn't say anything.

When they moved to the work table to make Noah's ark pictures, Mrs Lander gave each child a big piece of paper. Then she put some stiff cardboard shapes to draw round onto the middle of the table. There were animal shapes, a boat shape, and several people shapes.

'I'll do my picture,' said Anna-Magdalena to Neville who was next to her, 'then I'll help you do yours.'

Anna-Magdalena waited to see the very smallest of nods, but even though she carefully watched there wasn't a nod. In fact, she thought that maybe Neville shook his head to say 'no' but she wasn't sure.

Neville took a stack of animal shapes and looked at them. He looked at the elephant and put it back on the table. He looked at the giraffe and the tiger and put them back on the table. He put back the lion, the monkey and the bear. Some of the other children began to watch Neville putting all the shapes down.

'I want to have *lots* of lions and tigers and bears in my picture,' said Jack.

'It's s'posed to be only two of each animal,' Anna-Magdalena pointed out. Then turning to Neville, she said, 'You wait and I'll help you.'

But Neville took no notice of Anna-Magdalena. At the bottom of the stack of animals he found a cow and a pig. He took the two shapes and drew neatly round them. Then, pushing the animal shapes aside, he began to draw by himself. Without any shapes to help, he drew two lambs. He drew two chickens. He drew two goats and two ducks.

Neville never looked up. He drew around the boat shape for the ark. Then he drew a sort of ramp, for the animals to get into the boat. Then he drew one cat sitting on the ark and another on the ramp. Finally he drew wavy lines along the bottom of the boat for the water.

Jack leaned over the table to look at Neville's drawing. 'That's a good picture,' he said admiringly.

Anna-Magdalena leaned over to look too. Then all the children leaned over to see Neville's picture.

'That's a lovely picture, Neville,' said Mrs Lander. 'You've picked all the farm animals to draw, haven't you? Because you've lived on a farm, you know just what they look like.'

Neville gave a little nod.

Then Mrs Lander turned to the rest of the class.

'This month it's our turn to display our pictures on the walls of the church hall, so *all* of your pictures will be put up for people to see.'

Then she held up a little magazine. 'One more thing,' she added, smiling, 'the very best picture of all will be printed in our church magazine with your name beside it.'

'Neville's,' cried Anna-Magdalena. 'Neville's is the best picture.'

'Neville, Neville,' joined in Jack. That's nice of Jack, thought Anna-Magdalena, because his picture was probably the next best one. Then all the other children joined in and said that Neville's picture should be chosen.

Turning to the silent little boy, Mrs Lander asked, 'Would you like your picture in the magazine, Neville?'

Neville gave not the very smallest of nods, not even a medium-sized nod, but a very big nod indeed.

Anna-Magdalena tugged at Neville's sleeve. 'My picture's gone a bit wrong, Neville,' she said. 'Will you help me do a new one?'

Neville stared at her. Then his face broke into a huge smile. It was the first Neville smile that anyone had ever seen.

The class was even more surprised when Neville opened his mouth and said to Anna-Magdalena, 'Yes, I'll help you.' And he gave the very biggest nod that anyone had ever seen.

4
Anna-Magdalena
Goes to the Wedding

One day Anna-Magdalena was busy making 'chocolate' mud pies on the garden path. She had a small pan of water and a scoop to dig up the earth. She sprinkled just enough water onto a scoopful of earth to make stiff mud that would roll nicely into a ball. Then she thumped the ball flat into a neat, round shape on the path. So far she had made four 'chocolate' pies.

As she dug a fifth scoopful of earth, she heard the back door open and close and the sound of her mum's feet coming up the path.

'Mags, I have a special favour to ask,' said her mum.

'OK,' said Anna-Magdalena agreeably, busily decorating each 'chocolate' pie with a 'cherry' pebble.

'One day next month I would like you to wear a dress,' her mum said. 'It's for an important occasion,' she added.

A dress! Anna-Magdalena's face fell. She gave the newest pie an extra hard thump.

Anna-Magdalena was a small, determined person who *did not* like dresses. She liked jeans and dungarees. She liked shorts. She liked trousers. But she did not like dresses. People in dresses were sometimes not allowed to do interesting things, like washing the car or digging for worms. She was going to dig for worms that very afternoon with her big friend Gerald and then go fishing. She couldn't do interesting things like that in a dress.

'Why do I need a dress?' Anna-Magdalena asked. She blew her straight, orange fringe off her forehead, a sure sign that she was worried.

Her mother sat down on the step nearby and took a deep breath. 'Next month on the first Saturday, something very special will happen and I want you to be a big part of it. I want you to be a bridesmaid.'

'What's a bridesmaid?' asked Anna-Magdalena. She was collecting small pieces of grass to sprinkle on the pies for coconut topping.

'A bridesmaid,' replied her mum, 'is someone who helps the bride and groom in the church service when they are getting married.'

Anna-Magdalena pricked up her ears. She liked weddings, especially the food afterwards.

'A bridesmaid is what I want you to be for Gerald and me,' continued her mum, 'because we are going to get married.'

'Oh!' said Anna-Magdalena, her blue eyes widening in surprise.

'Then after the wedding, Gerald will live here with us and be like a daddy for you,' said her mum, patting her lap and looking at Anna-Magdalena.

Anna-Magdalena came over and sat on her mum's lap.

'But my daddy is the one in the big picture,' said Anna-Magdalena.

'I know, my love, but your daddy died, and he's in heaven with God now. You know we've talked about it before.'

'But I didn't want him to die,' said Anna-Magdalena.

'Neither did I,' said her mum. 'But God knows all about us, he loves us, and he is looking after us.'

Anna-Magdalena's mum reached into the pocket of her jeans and took out a tissue. She wiped a big muddy mark off Anna-Magdalena's chin.

Her mum said, 'You know, when I marry Gerald and have a new husband, it doesn't mean that I'll forget your daddy. I only have to look at your bright hair to think of him—his was just that colour.'

'Is it a nice colour?' Anna-Magdalena wanted to know.

Her mother gave her a squeeze. 'It's a very nice colour.'

'Will Gerald still take me fishing and to the swings in the park when he lives here?' asked Anna-Magdalena. 'And can I wash my hands?'

Her mum laughed. 'Of course, to both questions. Let's leave the mud pies . . . '

'*Chocolate*,' interrupted Anna-Magdalena.

'Sorry. Let's leave the *chocolate* pies to bake in the sun and let's get you cleaned up for lunch.'

As Anna-Magdalena finished scrubbing her hands, her mum brought a clean T-shirt into the bathroom.

'What did you say I'd be?' asked Anna-Magdalena.

'A bridesmaid. There's going to be a special service in our church. Gerald and I will stand at the front and promise to love and care for each other. You will stand with us in a pretty dress holding flowers.'

'I can hold flowers in shorts,' said Anna-Magdalena firmly.

Her mum laughed and tickled her. 'Mags,' she said, 'I've had an idea about your dress—you leave it to me.'

The day of the wedding dawned bright and clear. Anna-Magdalena and her mum were up early. After breakfast of scrambled egg and toast with strawberry jam, they got themselves ready for the wedding. Anna-Magdalena's mum dressed in a pale blue suit, then Anna-Magdalena put on a new outfit of the same blue with a yellow-and-blue-striped jacket. The yellow matched the flowers she was going to carry.

'OK?' asked her mum.

'OK,' Anna-Magdalena nodded.

When they were ready, Aunty Cath and Uncle Henry picked them up and drove them to the church. Gerald was waiting outside and he hurried over as their car pulled up. He gave Anna-Magdalena a quick hug as she got out of the car and then took her mum's hand.

'Come on, my two favourite girls. It's almost time,' he said.

Anna-Magdalena concentrated on holding her flowers nicely during the service and remembered not to fidget or look behind at the people in the church.

Afterwards, Anna-Magdalena's mother and Aunty Cath were laughing and crying and had their arms around each other while Gerald shook hands with Uncle Henry.

Then Uncle Henry said to Anna-Magdalena, 'Well, well, Sausage, I never thought to see *you* in a dress.'

'It's not a dress,' said Anna-Magdalena and her mother together.

'See!' said Anna-Magdalena. And she ran to the railing at the side of the path and hung upside down, demonstrating beyond any doubt that the pretty blue dress was not a dress at all. It was culottes, which only looked like a dress. Anna-Magdalena called them 'big shorts'.

'Well, well, Sausage,' said Uncle Henry again. 'You had *me* fooled.

Anna-Magdalena just gave a big upside-down grin.

Afterwards at the wedding lunch, Gerald gave a little speech. He thanked Anna-Magdalena for being the best bridesmaid he'd ever seen—and also the only one he'd ever seen wearing 'big shorts'.

5
Anna-Magdalena
Goes Glug-Glug-Glug

One morning Anna-Magdalena went out into the garden to tell Granny Charles some good news.

Granny Charles who lived next door was Anna-Magdalena's special friend. Granny was well again after being in hospital with a bump on her head and a broken wrist. The plaster cast which had held the wrist firmly while it was mending was off now too.

Anna-Magdalena looked through the gap in the hedge to wave at Granny. And there she was, just where she should be, sitting by the window reading her Bible.

'Granny Charles, Granny Charles—it's me, Anna-Magdalena,' she called out.

Granny looked up and waved. Then she unlatched and opened the window.

'Look, Anna-Magdalena, I can knit again,' said

Granny, pointing to the ball of blue wool and two knitting needles lying on the table. 'My old wrist is so much stronger I can do this.' Granny turned her hand round and round in small circles.

Anna-Magdalena watched and then tried out her own hand in small circles. Yes, hers was working well, too.

'Thank you for praying for me, Anna-Magdalena,' said Granny. 'Your mother told me that you did.'

Anna-Magdalena nodded. 'Every night I said, "Please, dear Jesus, make Granny Charles well again."'

Granny said smiling, 'And now I am. Do you want to come in for milk and a biscuit?'

Then Anna-Magdalena remembered the good news she'd come to tell.

'I can't,' she said. 'I've got my first swimming lesson.'

She jumped up and down with excitement at the thought.

'That's wonderful,' said Granny Charles. 'I didn't know you were keen on swimming.'

Anna-Magdalena nodded. 'I'm going on holiday with Aunty Cath and Uncle Henry. There's a lake and I want to swim and swim and swim every day.'

Anna-Magdalena made swimming strokes in the air with her arms and kicked first one foot and then the other. She added, 'Mum and Gerald aren't coming.

They're going on a honeypot.'

'A what?' asked Granny. She was puzzled.

'A honeypot,' Anna-Magdalena explained, 'It's a holiday after a wedding. They didn't have one because Gerald couldn't leave work.'

Granny Charles chuckled. 'I think you mean a honey*moon*.'

'Yes, that's it,' Anna-Magdalena smiled too.

Her mum called from the door. 'Mags, say good-bye to Granny. It's nearly time to go.'

Anna-Magdalena waved goodbye to her friend and ran into the house to get ready.

It took about ten minutes on the bus to get to the swimming baths.

Anna-Magdalena put on her new green swimsuit in the changing room and went to stand with some other children by the pool. They were in the beginners' class. Her mum sat down on a bench with the other parents at one side of the pool.

Soon a tall, strong-looking, dark-haired girl in a blue swimsuit and flipflops came out of a side door. She walked over to the little group of children.

'Hallo,' she said. 'My name is Pat. I'm your teacher. We're going to have a good time together. And we're all going to learn to swim, aren't we?'

'Yes-s-s-s,' chorused the children, including Anna-Magdalena.

Pat asked the children to stand in a line at the end of

the pool. She walked down the line and asked their names.

Then Pat asked all the children to sit down on the side of the pool and dangle their legs into the water.

'Now kick your legs in the water,' she said.

Anna-Magdalena kicked up a tremendous splash and so did the girl next to her. Her name was Geeta.

'Now,' said Pat, sitting down on the side of the pool, 'slide yourselves over the edge into the water like this. It isn't cold and it isn't deep.'

All the children slid gently into the pool. Anna-Magdalena was the smallest in the class and the water came just below her shoulders.

'All right, everybody out,' called Pat. 'Climb up the ladder and we'll do that again.'

All the children lined up at the side of the pool. They dangled their feet in the water. They kicked very hard. They slid gently into the pool. Anna-Magdalena splashed Geeta. Geeta splashed Anna-Magdalena. This was not part of the lesson.

'Now,' said Pat, 'don't splash each other. Climb up the ladder again, all of you.'

The children lined up again.

'This time,' Pat said, 'I'm going to hold your hands like this.' And she held Anna-Magdalena's hands. 'And you're going to jump in. Like this.'

Anna-Magdalena jumped in, making a terrific splash. She was glad Pat was holding her hands, but the fizzy, splashy feeling of the water was lovely. She turned round and waved to her mum. She *liked* swimming lessons.

One by one, all the children jumped in with an enormous splash. Then the lesson was over.

'I *like* swimming,' said Anna-Magdalena happily as her mum rubbed her dry with a big towel. 'I can do everything,' she said.

Anna-Magdalena just couldn't wait to go swimming again. This time, after the children all jumped into the water, Pat asked them to scoop water up and get their faces wet. Next, she showed them how to put their faces in the water for just a moment. There was a bit of spluttering, but they all did that. And, one by one, Pat pulled them gently across the pool, holding their arms, while they kicked their legs.

'Very good, Anna-Magdalena,' said Pat. 'You're doing well.'

Anna-Magdalena bounced up and down in the water with happiness.

The next lesson came and Pat showed the children how to lie on their backs in the water. 'If you let it, the water will hold you,' she explained. 'It's called floating.'

She held each child in turn, and when they were floating let them go for just a tiny moment.

When she got to Anna-Magdalena, Pat held her gently. Anna-Magdalena looked up at the ceiling. It

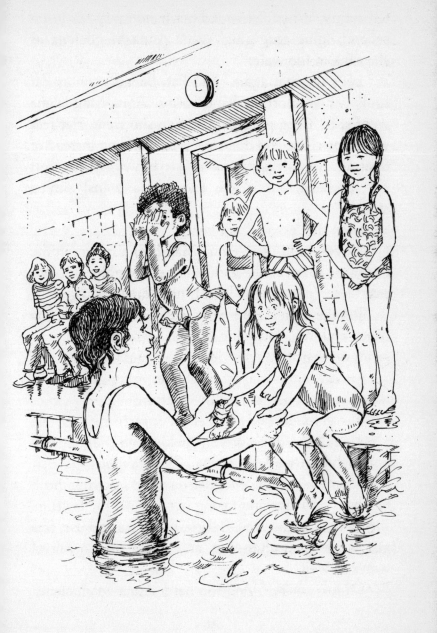

felt funny. When Pat tookd her hand away for just a second, 'glug-glug-glug' went Anna-Magdalena as she sank in the water.

'Let's try that again,' said Pat. But as soon as Pat took her supporting hand away, Anna-Magdalena went stiff. 'Glug-glug-glug', down she went. Her feet went down too and there she was, standing instead of floating. Anna-Magdalena tried to blow her fringe off her forehead, but it was too wet and just stayed stuck.

Then the lesson was over.

'Never mind,' said Anna-Magdalena's mum in the changing room as she looked at her daughter's downcast face. 'I'm sure you'll do it next time.'

But she didn't. And what was worse, some of the other children, including Geeta, were beginning to swim on their tummies, doing doggy-paddle.

Anna-Magdalena just went 'glug-glug-glug' every time she took her feet off the bottom.

'Never mind,' said Pat. 'Let's try practising with just your legs,' and, as before, she held Anna-Magdalena's arms while Anna-Magdalena kicked her legs.

Whenever Anna-Magdalena tried moving both her arms and legs and taking her feet off the bottom, she made a tremendous splash, but it was no use. She just went 'glug-glug-glug' and got a mouth full of water as well.

'I think you're trying too hard, Anna-Magdalena,'

said Pat. 'Let the water hold you. Some people just don't float as easily as others but they can certainly learn to swim.'

That night when Anna-Magdalena said her prayers, she asked Jesus to help her learn to swim. Her mum said gently, 'Ask him to help you to be patient while you learn.'

The next three lessons were the same. Anna-Magdalena could jump into the water. She could kick at the side. She could kick behind a white foam board. She could paddle around in her armbands. But when she tried all on her own, she went 'glug-glug-glug'. And she ended up standing instead of swimming.

Before long, all the children were swimming a little bit, except Anna-Magdalena. She tried to be glad for them, but it wasn't easy.

Suddenly, there was no more time to learn to swim. The day had come for Anna-Magdalena's holiday at the lake with Aunty Cath and Uncle Henry. Gerald and Anna-Magdalena's mum were all packed and ready to go on their special holiday that Anna-Magdalena remembered now to call a honeymoon.

'Well, well, Sausage,' said Uncle Henry when he and Aunty Cath arrived to collect Anna-Magdalena. 'I hope you've brought your swimsuit because we'll be doing lots of swimming at the lake.'

Anna-Magdalena burst into tears. After she told Uncle Henry all about her swimming lessons, he said kindly, 'Don't you worry, Sausage, we'll go wading round the edge, you and I. We'll dig for worms and do some fishing. We'll find one of those pedal boat things and go pedalling in the shallow bit.'

Anna-Magdalena dried her tears and began to smile. She thought, I can't paddle but I know how to pedal.

The weather was fine all week long. Uncle Henry, Anna-Magdalena and Aunty Cath did all the things he said they'd do, and many more.

On the last day of a happy week, Uncle Henry said to Anna-Magdalena that she was to put on her swimsuit and come with him.

They walked down to the lake and waded in.

'I want you to try something, Sausage,' said Uncle Henry. 'Lie back in the water. That's right, on your back. I'll hold you while you get comfortable.'

Anna-Magdalena smiled at Uncle Henry. It was different swimming in a lake with the big sky above.

'Pretend you're floating on a raft, a sort of boat,' said Uncle Henry. 'It's a big blue raft. Feel how the soft raft holds you up. You're drifting along on this raft until you come to a nice little cove that has an ice cream stall.'

Anna-Magdalena grinned and relaxed. She could feel Uncle Henry's hands holding her. Drifting and ice cream, this was nice. 'Can I have chocolate?' she enquired.

'Absolutely,' said Uncle Henry. 'Remember to keep drifting, though.'

After a while she saw Uncle Henry raise one hand from the water. Then, a moment later, he raised the other hand.

'There you are, Sausage,' said Uncle Henry. 'You're floating all on your own on your raft of water.'

That afternoon, at last, Anna-Magdalena floated and floated and smiled and smiled and she didn't go 'glug-glug-glug' even once.

6

Anna-Magdalena and the Creepy Crawly

Anna-Magdalena was lying on her tummy on the carpet in the sitting room. She was drawing a picture for Gerald, her new daddy. He'd told Anna-Magdalena that he would like something nice to put on his wall at work.

She called to her mum in the kitchen. 'Shall I draw you and me and Sam in the garden?'

Sam was Anna-Magdalena's guinea-pig. She always checked every morning to see if he showed signs of growing a tail. But she had been looking and waiting for a long time now and she was beginning to lose hope.

'I know,' Anna-Magdalena said to herself, 'I'll *draw* a tail for Sam.'

Anna-Magdalena was a small, determined person who did not give up on an idea easily.

'Mum,' she called again, 'I'm going to draw a tail for Sam.'

'That's nice,' said her mum.

I don't think she's listening, thought Anna-Magdalena. But I'll draw it and show her when I'm finished. She picked up two crayons and drew a round, black-and-white shape for Sam. She was just adding a swishy, long stroke for a lovely tail when she caught sight of something out of the corner of her eye.

It was large and black. It had a lot of legs. It was running across the floor.

Anna-Magdalena screamed. For her small size, she had a very very large voice. She gave a little shiver and screamed again. Then she began to cry.

Her mum rushed in from the kitchen. 'Mags, what's the matter?'

She scooped Anna-Magdalena up into her arms and they sat down together on the sofa. Her mum hugged her tight and patted her and said, 'It's all right. It's all right.'

Finally, between hiccups and sobs, Anna-Magdalena told what she'd seen.

She said, 'It was big and horrible —it had a hundred legs—it was black—it was running right after me —it was going to get me.' She shivered again.

'Poor Mags,' said her mum. 'You've had quite a scare. I know what you've seen, I think. It's a very big spider. I saw it too, the other day.'

Anna-Magdalena was surprised. 'You saw it. Did you cry?'

Her mum smiled. 'Well, no,' she said. 'I know it looks large and scary, but it won't hurt you.'

Mum pointed to the skirting board at the bottom of the wall. 'I think it lives under there.'

Anna-Magdalena was not pleased to hear this news. She blew the straight orange fringe off her forehead.

Mum said, 'Every house—and every garden too—has got spiders. Come with me. I've got something to show you.'

But first, they washed the tears off Anna-Magdalena's face. Then they chose two shiny red apples to eat. At last, they went into the garden for what her mum called 'a creepy-crawly tour'.

Anna-Magdalena held her mum's hand very tightly. Her mum said, 'It's a wonderful world God has made for us. There are animals as big as elephants. Remember the one we saw at the zoo?'

Anna-Magdalena nodded. She remembered the huge, grey animal with the long, swinging trunk.

Her mum continued, 'And there are animals even smaller than that ant.'

Her mum pointed to the path. Anna-Magdalena looked down to watch a tiny ant scurrying along a crack.

'There are big spiders like the one you saw,' said her

mum, 'and there are little spiders.' She added, 'There are even pretty speckled spiders. See, on this bush.'

Anna-Magdalena crept forward cautiously. When she got very near, she saw a tiny creature no bigger than her little fingernail. The little spider was sitting on a leaf. He didn't look a bit frightening.

Anna-Magdalena's mum asked, 'By the way, how many legs did you say your big spider had?'

'Lots and lots,' said Anna-Magdalena. And she looked down at the little speckled spider to see if *it* had lots and lots.

Her mum said, 'All spiders have eight legs. That's lots and lots compared to you and me. Mags, your two legs and my two legs make only half a spider.'

Anna-Magdalena giggled at the idea. Her mum laughed too and then said, 'All these different creatures are part of God's world. Elephants and ants and guinea-pigs and spiders and—people! God loves us all.'

They walked to the end of the garden. Anna-Magdalena's mum promised that they would see something really beautiful.

It was a misty autumn morning. It was just the right time, her mum said, to see the garden spider's home. And there it was. It was strung over two low-growing shrubs. It was a sort of circular pattern of threads covered in tiny drops of water. It sparkled and glittered in the light. It was lovely.

Anna-Magdalena's mum said, 'This is the garden spider's home and work place. It's a web. The spider makes thread out of its own body and builds the web always the same way.'

Anna-Magdalena studied the pretty web pattern. 'What's it for?' she asked.

Her mum said, 'It's sticky in the middle and flies get stuck on it. Then the spider eats the flies.'

Anna-Magdalena touched a gentle finger to the edge of the web. 'Does the spider get stuck on his web too?' she asked.

Her mum explained how the stronger lines leading to the centre of the web weren't sticky and that the spider moved backwards and forwards on those.

'Where's the spider now?' Anna-Magdalena wanted to know.

They looked around the edge of the web. They had to look rather hard and then Anna-Magdalena spotted a ginger-coloured spider. He wasn't quite as tiny as the little speckled creature they'd seen earlier. But this spider wasn't frightening either.

'What if I broke the web?' asked Anna-Magdalena putting out a testing finger again.

'He'd just get busy and repair it. But it's so beautiful, let's not do that,' said her mum. 'Spiders eat quite a few garden pests, so they're really good things to have around.'

That night when Gerald came home from work, he

was pleased with the garden picture Anna-Magdalena had made. There was Anna-Magdalena and her mum and Sam, the guinea-pig. There was also a small, round brown blob with eight legs in one corner.

'What's this, then, Mags?' asked Gerald, ruffling her hair and pointing to the brown blob.

'It's a spider,' Anna-Magdalena answered, and she told him about her scare and the 'creepy crawly tour' outside. 'But I'm not scared any more,' she said to him. Then she added that her mum thought spiders were good things to have around.

'Oh, she thinks that, does she?' enquired Gerald raising his eyebrows. He winked at Anna-Magdalena. 'I have a little plan for you and me. I've just seen something interesting in a toy shop.' And he whispered in her ear.

The next night after Anna-Magdalena and her mum had said their prayers together, Anna-Magdalena climbed into bed for a bedtime story.

She said, 'I want a different book tonight, please.'

'OK,' agreed her mum, putting the usual book back on the shelf and taking the half-opened book Anna-Magdalena handed to her. When her mum opened the book to read the story, she suddenly screamed 'AARGH!' and jumped, dropping the book onto the bed.

There, hopping on the book's pages was a large, furry. . . toy spider. Attached to the toy spider was a

58

green tube. The green tube went from the spider into a little round rubber bulb in Anna-Magdalena's hand. When she squeezed the bulb, it pushed air into the spider and made it hop.

'Oh, Mags—you did make me jump,' said her mum. 'You and Gerald have been shopping today, I see,' and she laughed a little breathlessly. 'I *thought* you two went to the park.'

Gerald appeared in the doorway laughing too and put his arm around Anna-Magdalena's mum.

'Well,' he said, 'you did say... what was it, Mags?'

Anna-Magdalena and Gerald recited together, 'Spiders are good things to have around.'

Anna-Magdalena curled up in a fit of giggles and laughed so hard she fell out of bed.

7
Anna-Magdalena
Wants a Baby Brother

One winter morning Anna-Magdalena pressed her nose against the cold glass of the front window. Wherever she looked it was white. It had snowed all night and even now a few flakes continued to drift down.

Anna-Magdalena called, 'Mummy, it's snowed! I want to go out.'

After breakfast, Anna-Magdalena and her mum each put on thick trousers, two pairs of warm socks, two woolly sweaters, a warm jacket, scarf, hat, mittens, and wellingtons.

Wearing so many clothes, Anna-Magdalena was almost square in shape and could hardly move at all at first. She couldn't even blow her fringe aside, as it was tucked up under her hat.

They went out into the white world. First they built

a little snowman. They pressed pieces of coal into the snow for his eyes and mouth and used a carrot for a nose. They added an old hat and scarf and he looked quite smart.

Then they made angels in the snow. Anna-Magdalena found some clean, unmarked snow in the back garden. She lay down on her back and fanned her arms in the snow up over her head and down to her sides to make the angel's wings. Then she stood up carefully so she didn't spoil the outline. It was a good angel shape, she thought. She made three angels in a row. Then her mum lay down in the snow to add a big angel to lie beside the little ones.

'We're all snowy now,' said Anna-Magdalena's mum. 'Shall we go in?'

'Aren't you going to do the paths?' asked Anna-Magdalena. 'I'll help.' She had a little scoop that she wanted to try out.

'The snow is too heavy,' said her mum. 'We'll leave it for Gerald to clear when he comes home.'

'What about Granny Charles?' asked Anna-Magdalena. 'You did her path last time.'

Her mum shook her head. 'No, it's too heavy for me now. Gerald will do her path when he does ours. Come inside —it's time I told you something.'

All the snowy, wet clothes were hung up in the back hall, and Anna-Magdalena helped her mum make cocoa. They floated a marshmallow on the top of each steaming mug of chocolate. It tasted delicious.

'Now then,' said Anna-Magdalena's mum, as they settled themselves at the kitchen table, 'I've got something exciting to tell you.'

What could it be, Anna-Magdalena wondered. Were they going to get a new kitten?

Her mum continued, 'The exciting thing is, that God has given us something very special. Our family—you and I and Gerald—are going to have a baby. You are going to have a little sister or a little brother in the summer!'

A sister or brother! Anna-Magdalena's mouth fell open in surprise.

'Where is it now?' she asked.

Her mum patted her own tummy. 'The baby's in here. That's why I have to be a little careful and not shovel heavy snow. The baby is still very small, only about this size.' She put her two little fingers end to end to show Anna-Magdalena about how long the baby was. Then she told Anna-Magdalena that the baby was growing all the time and soon her tummy would look rounder and fatter.

Anna-Magdalena's mum said, 'We'll have a good time, you and I, getting ready for the new baby. The next time we go to the shops, you can choose a new, soft little toy to hang in the cot.'

That evening when Gerald came home, Anna-Magdalena met him at the door to tell him her news.

'We're having a baby!' she cried.

He didn't seem surprised, but picked her up to give her a hug. 'It's terrific news, isn't it?' he said.

'I thought about it all day,' said Anna-Magdalena. 'I decided we want a boy.' She looked at him anxiously and blew her fringe off her forehead. 'Is that all right?'

Then she explained that they didn't need a girl as they already had one. What their family needed was a boy.

'Mags,' said Gerald, 'a baby, any baby, is a very special gift from God. We can't choose. We'll be happy with a boy *or* a girl.'

'But a girl might want to wear dresses,' she said worriedly. At that moment Anna-Magdalena couldn't think of anything worse than a little sister who would wear dresses and want Anna-Magdalena to play dolls.

Gerald gave a great shout of laughter. 'Fat chance,' he said, 'of any little sister of *yours* being allowed to wear dresses.' He chuckled again and scooped Anna-Magdalena up to give her a piggyback ride into the kitchen.

The next evening when Gerald came in from work, Anna-Magdalena again met him at the front door.

'I thought about the baby all day,' she said. 'I want him to have black hair.'

'It's all right with me,' answered Gerald, smiling. 'Like me, you mean?'

Anna-Magdalena looked at him carefully and then

she nodded.

'OK,' said Gerald. 'Can you work on a name next?'

A name for the baby proved quite a problem for Anna-Magdalena. She wanted a short name so that everyone would call the baby by his real right name. No Anna-Banana, Mags, Maggy-Waggy nicknames for her little brother, she had decided!

As the weeks passed, she asked about all the names she heard on the radio or on television or from people talking.

One morning Anna-Magdalena and her mum were washing down Anna-Magdalena's old cot that Gerald had brought down from the attic. 'Bob is a good name,' she said. It was a name she'd heard on the radio that morning.

Her mum answered, 'That's really Robert and often becomes Robbie or Rob or Bobby.'

'Oh,' said Anna-Magdalena. She had already tried out 'Tim'. It was short for Timothy. 'Ted' was short for Edward. 'Nick' was short for Nicholas. 'Tom' was short for Thomas. 'Bill' was short for William.

Anna-Magdalena crawled out from under the cot where she had been wiping off the cot legs with a cloth. 'Aren't *any* names what they are?' she complained.

Her mum laughed and sat down on a little stool. Her tummy looked very round now and there was no room for Anna-Magdalena to sit on her lap. She sat on the floor at her mum's feet instead.

'Mags, I'm sure we'll think of a good name in the end. But please remember that the baby could be a girl. I don't want you to be disappointed. Shall we think of some girl's names?'

'He's a boy,' said Anna-Magdalena. She felt sure it was true. 'With black hair,' she added. Anna-Magdalena was a very determined person. She could picture this baby in her mind.

Her mum sighed. 'Oh dear. Well, what about George? That's not short for anything?'

'Georgy-Porgy,' cried Anna-Magdalena, remembering the nursery rhyme about the boy who kissed the girls and made them cry. 'Oh no —not George,' she said.

Some weeks later, Anna-Magdalena, her mum and Gerald were painting in the tiny room they were getting ready for the new baby. The two grown-ups were painting the room a lovely lemon yellow. Anna-Magdalena was painting a cardboard box for the baby to put his toys in. She was painting it red.

'Do you like Chris?' asked Anna-Magdalena, returning to the name game.

Her mum answered, 'It's short for Christopher.'

Gerald looked over his shoulder and winked. 'Or Christine,' he said.

'Oh no,' said Anna-Magdalena.

Gerald put down his paintbrush and went to

inspect Anna-Magdalena's work. He nodded at the smoothly painted bright red box. Anna-Magdalena's hands were also a smooth, bright red.

'You know, Mags, *if* it's a boy I would like to call him after my father, perhaps for a middle name. My father's name was Matthew—it's a special name in the Bible too.'

Anna-Magdalena considered the name 'Matthew'. It was rather long. 'Why is Matthew special?' she wanted to know.

Gerald stood up and went back to his painting. He said, 'Matthew was one of the special four people who told all the good things that Jesus said and did. The others were Mark, Luke and John.'

Anna-Magdalena's face lit up. Three more short names. She questioned the two grown-ups.

They said that Mark could be short for Marcus. John had lots and lots of nicknames.

'What about Luke,' asked Anna-Magdalena. 'What's it short for?'

But nobody knew any other names for Luke. It seemed that people called Luke were called Luke.

Gerald said to Anna-Magdalena's mum. 'What about Luke Matthew?'

She smiled. 'I like it.'

'I like it too,' cried Anna-Magdalena. 'I will call him *just* Luke.'

'*If* it's a boy,' her mum warned.

'I wish he'd hurry up,' said Anna-Magdalena.

One warm summer night several weeks later, Anna-Magdalena woke up in the middle of the night. Aunty Cath was there instead of her mum and Gerald. The baby was on its way, Aunty Cath told her. Her mum and Gerald were at the hospital.

Next morning as Anna-Magdalena was eating her cereal and toast with honey, the phone rang. Aunty Cath went to answer it and Anna-Magdalena heard her say, 'That's wonderful news.'

'What do you think, Mags?' said Aunty Cath. 'The baby's here and . . .'

'It's a boy!' Aunty Cath and Anna-Magdalena said together. Anna-Magdalena said delightedly, 'I *knew* it.'

Aunty Cath grabbed Anna-Magdalena's hands and they danced round and round the kitchen singing, 'It's a boy—it's a boy—it's a brand new boy!'

When they stopped, Anna-Magdalena asked, 'Has he got black hair?'

Aunty Cath replied rather breathlessly, 'I'm sorry, I never asked. Your mum will be home with him the day after tomorrow. You can see for yourself.'

But when Anna-Magdalena had her first look at her little brother, she had a surprise. He didn't have black hair. He didn't have brown hair. He didn't have orange hair. He didn't have blond hair. He didn't have any hair at all!

8

Anna-Magdalena Doesn't Want a Baby Brother

Anna-Magdalena, eyes bright with excitement, raced into the house from the garden.

'Mummy, mummy,' she shouted. 'Did you know ...?'

Her mum put a finger to her lips to say 'Shush', but it was too late. The new baby, Anna-Magdalena's little brother, had been about to drop off to sleep in his mother's arms. Now his eyes snapped open and he began to cry.

'Waah, waah,' he bawled. Little Luke was very small but he could make a very large noise.

'Oh, Mags,' said her mum, 'do try to remember not to shout when it's his naptime.' Tiredly, she rubbed her free hand over her eyes. 'He woke up several times in the night. I was hoping he'd have a good long sleep this morning so *I* could rest.'

Anna-Magdalena, her happy news forgotten for the moment, said crossly, 'Why does Luke cry all the time?'

Her mum put Luke on her shoulder and patted his back. He continued to cry noisily. She raised her voice so that her older child could hear over the wailing baby.

'He doesn't cry *all* the time. He has to cry sometimes because that's how he tells me he's hungry or tired or too hot or needs his nappy changed.'

'Well, I get tired of him crying,' said Anna-Magdalena. Then she brightened as she remembered what she'd come in to tell.

'Granny Charles has kittens!' she announced. Then Anna-Magdalena told her mum about the large black-and-white cat that Granny Charles next door had found in her garden. The cat seemed to be lost, so Granny had been feeding it while trying to find its owner. Then to her surprise, last night, four kittens had been born. Granny Charles had just told Anna-Magdalena all about it through the gap in the hedge.

'They're in Granny's kitchen. Can we go and see them?' Anna-Magdalena looked up at her mum hopefully.

'I'll call Granny and see if it's all right for you to make a visit. *I'll* come another time when Luke isn't so unsettled,' said Anna-Magdalena's mum.

After a quick phone call, Anna-Magdalena slipped

through the hedge and tapped on Granny's back door.

'Come in, Anna-Magdalena,' said Granny, opening the door. 'Come in and see my new family.'

Anna-Magdalena ran to a cardboard box in the corner of the kitchen. Inside, lying on a soft, thick cloth, was the black-and-white cat. She was purring as four very tiny kittens nuzzled at her tummy where they were feeding.

The kittens were much smaller than Anna-Magdalena had been expecting. 'I brought a ball for them to play with,' she said, peering into the box. She took a little ball from the pocket of her jeans.

'They can't play yet,' said Granny, 'but I'll keep the ball for them. They don't open their eyes for a week or so. Then they have to grow a bit before they're ready to play.'

Anna-Magdalena sat down beside the box to have a better view. Two of the kittens were black and white, one was ginger coloured, and one was a mixture of colours with a big orange patch on its head.

Anna-Magdalena said to herself, 'I wish I had a kitten and not a little brother.'

Granny looked at her kindly, but she didn't say anything.

About an hour later when Anna-Magdalena popped back through the hedge, she raced into the kitchen shouting, 'Mummy, mummy, you should see —'

Her mum put a finger to her lips to say 'Shush', but

again it was too late. The baby, who had been about to fall asleep in his carrycot, opened his eyes and began to cry.

'Waah, waah,' he bawled.

This time the baby was left to cry for a moment, and Anna-Magdalena was taken by the hand. Her mum led her into the sitting room and shut the door.

She said, 'I know it's hard to remember about being quiet because of Luke, but it's just for a little while. Soon he'll sleep well and it won't be a problem, I'm sure.'

Anna-Magdalena felt disappointed with the baby and also with herself. Tears slowly began to run down her cheeks.

'I—don't—like—our—baby,' she sobbed. 'He doesn't like me. He always cries. He can't play. He can't do anything. I wish God would take him back.'

Anna-Magdalena's mum sat down on the sofa. She gave her daughter a big hug and lifted her up onto her lap.

'God has given us Luke, and we want to look after him,' she said. 'We wouldn't really want to give him back, even if we could, because we love him. I know you're disappointed because he cries and doesn't know how to play.'

Anna-Magdalena nodded so vigorously that tears splashed down her front.

Her mum continued, 'It's just because he's so little,

73

but he's growing and changing all the time. Very soon Luke will smile his first real smile. Keep looking and see if you're the first one to see him smile.'

Anna-Magdalena wiped away her tears and promised she would keep looking.

Next day, after checking on Luke, who wasn't smiling yet, Anna-Magdalena went to visit the kittens. She asked Granny Charles if she could help name them.

Granny Charles explained that she hoped to be able to find good homes for all the kittens and that their new owners would give them names. But when she saw Anna-Magdalena's disappointed face, Granny patted her on the shoulder and said that they could give them friendly names just for now.

'Naming is heavy work,' added Granny. 'Had we better have milk and a chocolate biscuit to help us?'

Anna-Magdalena grinned and nodded.

Over the drink and biscuit, Granny and Anna-Magdalena decided that the mainly black kitten with a little white on its chest, should be Blackie. The other black—and—white kitten had four white paws. Anna-Magdalena called it Boots. The all-ginger kitten was Ginger, of course.

'Now what about the tortoiseshell, our little lady with the orange patch on her head?' asked Granny.

'Patch,' cried Anna-Magdalena.

'Perfect,' said Granny.

'Patch is my favourite,' said Anna-Magdalena. 'I wish she could play ball now.'

Granny Charles told her she would just have to be patient. 'It's God's way,' said Granny, 'to let little animals, like kittens and puppies, be very helpless when they're newborn. They need lots of their mother's care before they're strong enough to play. It's also true for human babies.'

Here she caught Anna-Magdalena's eye. Anna-Magdalena looked thoughtful. 'My visitor cat is a good mum,' said Granny and she rubbed the black-and-white cat's head. 'She hardly ever leaves her babies.'

'You wait and see. You'll be surprised how fast the kittens will grow up,' said Granny.

From then on, Anna-Magdalena did two special things every single day. She always checked to see if Luke was ready to smile yet. And she always paid a visit to the kittens.

The kittens grew quickly. Just over a week after they were born they opened their eyes. It happened all at once. One day all their eyes were shut. The next day every single kitten was starting to look around with greeny-yellow eyes.

'Soon,' said Granny, 'you can pick them up and hold them for just a minute or two.'

Anna-Magdalena slipped back through the hedge and raced in through her own back door. She was just

about to shout, 'Mummy, Mummy,' when she suddenly remembered Luke. She quieted her voice and
said 'Mummy' instead.

'Good girl. You remembered,' said her mum.

Then Anna-Magdalena told her about the kittens'
eyes. It was so exciting. Her mum listened carefully to
Anna-Magdalena's news.

Then she asked Anna-Magdalena to do her a little
favour. 'I'm just about to give Luke a bath,' she said.
'He's awake. Would you go and talk to him for a
minute while I fill the baby bath with water?'

Anna-Magdalena went into Luke's little bedroom.
He was lying on his back. He was awake but he wasn't
crying.

'Hi, Luke,' said Anna-Magdalena and the baby
turned his head towards her. She pressed her face
against the bars of the cot down at his level.

'Want to hear a song?' asked Anna-Magdalena.

The baby didn't say 'no' so she began to sing a song
she'd learned in Sunday school.

> Jesus loves me, this I know
> For the Bible tells me so
> Little ones to him belong
> They are weak but he is strong.
> Yes, Jesus loves me.
> Yes, Jesus loves me.
> Yes, Jesus loves me.
> The Bible tells me so.

Anna-Magdalena sang the song very nicely. She knew both the words and the tune very well.

It seemed the baby thought so too. Luke looked at her and appeared to be listening to her song. Then he did something he'd never done before. He smiled his very first real smile.

'Do you think we can be friends?' whispered Anna-Magdalena.

The baby smiled again.

'I think we can,' Anna-Magdalena said, smiling back.

9

Anna-Magdalena and the Polka Dots

Anna-Magdalena sat down at the kitchen table to eat her lunch. On her plate was a toasted cheese sandwich and sticks of carrot. Afterwards she was going to have orange slices and a tiny cake with chocolate icing and a walnut on top. Anna-Magdalena and her mum said a little prayer to thank God for the good food. It was indeed a very nice lunch, but Anna-Magdalena looked at it and shook her head.

'Mummy, I'm not hungry,' she said.

'Toasted cheese is one of your favourite things,' said her mum, surprised.

'My head hurts,' said Anna-Magdalena.

Her mum reached over and felt her forehead. It was very hot. 'You've got a temperature,' said her mum, and she went to get the thermometer from the bathroom cabinet.

She put the thermometer into Anna-Magdalena's mouth. Anna-Magdalena concentrated hard, trying to keep the slippery thermometer stuck under her tongue, as she'd been told.

After a minute or so, her mum took out the thermometer and looked at it. 'Thirty-eight degrees,' she said. 'Yes, you *have* got a temperature. To bed with you, young lady.'

Anna-Magdalena slept all afternoon and when she woke up, she felt ill and feverish and her mouth was dry. 'Mummy,' she called weakly. 'Can I have a drink?'

Her mum brought some cool orange juice which Anna-Magdalena drank down thirstily.

'Let's have a look at you,' her mum said. She gently touched Anna-Magdalena's head. It was still hot. She unbuttoned the animal-patterned pyjama top and exclaimed as she stared at Anna-Magdalena's chest.

Anna-Magdalena looked too and her eyes widened in surprise. 'Polka dots,' she cried.

Her chest was full of pink spots!

Her mum said, 'I think it's chicken-pox, but I'll phone the doctor and see for certain.' After a quick phone call, her mum returned to say that their doctor was going to be nearby on another call and she would look in to see Anna-Magdalena.

'Mmm, yes,' said Doctor Harris a little later. 'A very good crop of chicken-pox,' and she smiled at Anna-Magdalena. 'You'll feel much better in a day or two, but you can probably expect a lot more spots. Try very hard not to scratch them, so they don't become sore.'

The next morning Anna-Magdalena still felt hot and miserable. She blew her orange fringe off her aching forehead and shut her eyes again. She slept most of the day, waking only to drink some soup and later some fruit juice.

In the evening, Anna-Magdalena said she felt well enough to listen to a story. Gerald came in to read a book about a hamster who went exploring. Then they said a prayer together. They asked Jesus to comfort Anna-Magdalena while she felt ill and to make her well soon.

The next morning, as the doctor had said, Anna-Magdalena *did* feel much better. Her head was no longer hot nor her mouth dry.

But when she looked at herself, she had spots on her legs and spots on her arms. She got out of bed and looked into the mirror. Spots on her face, too.

'More polka dots,' said Anna-Magdalena cheerfully to her mum as she came into the bedroom. 'Can I stay up now? I feel better. I want to go and show Luke my polka dots.'

'I'm afraid you can't see Luke until your spots begin to get better,' said her mum. 'He's only little and we don't want him to catch chicken-pox, too.'

'Oh,' said Anna-Magdalena. 'Can I have Polly in to play, then? Polly's big.' Polly was one of her friends

from Sunday school.'

Her mum shook her head. 'Chicken-pox is very easy to catch, so you'll have to make do with Gerald and me for company for the time being. Luckily *we've* both had it.'

For the next few days Gerald and Anna-Magdalena's mum spent a lot of time with the polka-dot kid, as Gerald called her. He brought home some playdough in five different colours. They made little people —a blue man, a green woman, a yellow girl, a red boy and a purple baby. Anna-Magdalena put little red spots on the yellow girl. 'That's me,' she said. She added, 'I wish all the people were real so we could play together.'

Anna-Magdalena and her mum sang all the songs they knew. 'Old Macdonald Had a Farm' was a favourite. 'Miss Polly Had a Dolly Who Was Sick, Sick, Sick,' they sang lots of times. They sang 'This Little Light of Mine, I'm Going to Let it Shine.' The light was the good news about how much Jesus loved them, said Anna-Magdalena's mum. They acted out the song's story—trying to hide or blow out the light and then letting it shine again.

When Sunday came, Anna-Magdalena asked if she could go to Sunday school. She liked the stories from the Bible and she liked making things after the story. She always went to Sunday School.

But not this Sunday. 'Sorry, Mags,' her mum said. By now Anna-Magdalena was absolutely covered in spots. Added to the spots on her tummy, arms, legs and face were spots in her hair and on her hands and feet. And now they itched. Oh, how they itched!

Sometimes Anna-Magdalena jumped up and down to try and keep from scratching. The doctor had said it was important not to scratch.

Every night Anna-Magdalena prayed that the chicken-pox would go away soon and that she could be strong and not scratch.

To soothe the itching, Anna-Magdalena had warm baths with a few spoonfuls of special white powder. Her mum said the powder was called bicarbonate of soda and would help for a while. Anna-Magdalena's mum also dabbed on a pinky-white lotion called calamine that felt cool. Anna-Magdalena laughed when she looked in the mirror and saw her whitened face. She thought she looked like a clown.

But still she itched and she had to try so hard not to scratch.

One evening she was standing in the sitting room with her arms outstretched and wiggling her fingers very fast so as to not scratch with them. Her mum walked into the room followed by Gerald carrying a basket.

'We have a surprise for you, Mags,' said her mum. 'We both think you've been the bravest and best girl ever. You haven't complained and you've tried very hard to do what the doctor said.'

Anna-Magdalena was pleased and started to smile. For the moment, her itchiness was forgotten.

Gerald added, 'We think you need a playmate to help you get through the rest of the time with chicken-pox.'

Playmate? Anna-Magdalena was amazed. She couldn't have anyone in to play, could she?

Gerald set the basket he was carrying on the floor. He lifted the lid and invited Anna-Magdalena to take a peek.

Scrambling up the side of the basket was a little tortoiseshell kitten with an orange patch on its head.

'Patch!' cried Anna-Magdalena. It was her favourite kitten from next door, one of the four kittens born to Granny Charles' stray cat. 'Can I play with her?' asked Anna-Magdalena, already gathering the kitten into her arms.

'Not only that,' said her mum. 'She's yours.'

'Mine?' said Anna-Magdalena in wonder and delight.

'Your very own to keep and look after,' said Gerald. He laughed and added, 'And *she* can't catch chicken-pox!'

'Now I'm glad I've got polka dots,' said Anna-Magdalena happily.

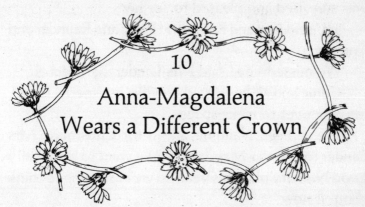

10
Anna-Magdalena Wears a Different Crown

Anna-Magdalena walked across the sitting room slowly trailing a piece of red string. Her kitten, Patch, pounced on the end of the string and tried to bite it. Anna-Magdalena pulled the string away and the kitten pounced again. It was a great game.

Anna-Magdalena's mum came into the room with her coat on. 'Time for Sunday school,' she said. 'Get your jacket, please.'

'Can I take Patch?' asked Anna-Magdalena. She didn't want to be parted from her new kitten for even a moment.

Her mum laughed and said 'no'.

Anna-Magdalena begged, 'Oh please, I'll keep her quiet.'

But her mum said 'no' more firmly, so Anna-Magdalena gave her kitten a cuddle and put her into her basket.

Anna-Magdalena hadn't been to Sunday school for three weeks while she had had chicken-pox. Everyone was surprised and pleased to see her.

'Hi,' said Jack and Kevin and Polly and Rajinder and Tommy.

'We missed you,' said Mrs Lander, her teacher.

'Come and sit here,' said Neville, her special friend, moving over to make space.

'We've been planning ahead for Christmas,' Mrs Lander told Anna-Magdalena. 'We want to do a really good Nativity play this year, so we're starting to think about it now.'

Anna-Magdalena knew from last year that the Nativity play would be about baby Jesus being born. She remembered the kings who came to see the baby. She broke in, excitedly, 'Can I be a king, please?'

Mrs Lander looked at her list. 'I'm sorry, Anna-Magdalena. Jack and two children from the other classes have been chosen for the kings. Would you like to be a shepherd instead?'

Anna-Magdalena's face fell. She did so want to wear a beautiful crown covered in gold or silver paper. All the kings last year had looked splendid in their crowns and had carried shining gifts for baby Jesus.

'I can't remember,' said Anna-Magdalena slowly, 'what do shepherds wear on their heads?'

Mrs Lander answered, 'We wrap round strips of

cloth, usually.'

'Oh,' said Anna-Magdalena. That *certainly* wasn't as good as a crown, she thought.

Mrs Lander saw Anna-Magdalena's disappointment, and she said kindly, 'Perhaps, as well as being a shepherd, you'd like to be my special play helper. It's quite a big job,' she added, encouragingly.

Anna-Magdalena nodded and tried to look pleased. But it was hard when what she really wanted to do was wear a crown.

Several weeks later the Sunday school children began to hear the story of the first Christmas. Mrs Lander told them how a long time ago, an angel came to see a young girl whose name was Mary. She was just an ordinary girl, but God had chosen her to be the mother of Jesus, God's own Son.

The children practised this scene for the play. Anna-Magdalena was very busy helping. Polly was playing the part of Mary. She sat quietly on a stool which Anna-Magdalena had covered with a cloth. Then an angel, a girl called Sarah from an older class, came to talk to Mary. Mrs Lander asked Anna-Magdalena to chalk a mark on the floor where the angel was to stand. Then Mary practised looking surprised and the angel practised telling the message about the baby.

Over the next two Sundays, the children continued

to learn about the Christmas story and to get ready for the play. Mrs Lander told how Mary and her new husband Joseph travelled to a town called Bethlehem. It was a long way and when Mary and Joseph got there, the town was full of people. It was time for Mary to have her baby, but there was nowhere to stay for the night.

When the children practised the journey and the search for a room, Kevin, who was Joseph, was especially good. He walked with slumped shoulders to show how tired he was.

Anna-Magdalena smiled at him and nodded her approval. As the special play helper, she concentrated really hard and soon found she was learning all the lines. Sometimes, without meaning to, she said the words quietly to herself along with the person who was speaking.

The next thing to happen in the Christmas story, said Mrs Lander, was the very best part. The only place Mary and Joseph could find to sleep was in a stable with farm animals. But it was warm and comfortable, and baby Jesus was born there. Mary wrapped him up and laid him on the straw in the animals' stall.

For the practice, Polly had brought her doll and Anna-Magdalena had brought one of her brother Luke's baby shawls. The cardboard figures for the animals weren't painted yet, so Anna-Magdalena said she would be a pretend cow. She mooed softly several times during the scene so that Polly and Kevin would feel they really were in a stable and not a Sunday school room.

Now came the shepherds' part and Anna-Magdalena joined in again. Acting out the story as Mrs Lander had told it, she and Neville and the other shepherds were afraid when an angel spoke to them. Anna-Magdalena blew her orange fringe off her forehead as she pretended to be frightened. But the angel said, 'Don't be afraid. I bring you good news. A baby has been born who has come to save all people.' The shepherds were very happy to hear this and hurried away. They were going to see the new baby.

Other people came to see him, too, Mrs Lander had told the children. Three wise men, or kings, came from the East, following a special star. God put it in the sky to lead them to the baby. When they found him, they knelt before him and gave him precious gifts.

Anna-Magdalena watched Jack and the other two kings get ready for this part of the play. They had to practise wearing crowns. Anna-Magdalena thought that the crowns were beautiful—one was gold, one was silver and one was covered with sparkling silver bits called glitter.

Anna-Magdalena pushed away a little bad thought and handed each king a gift to carry. 'Hold it carefully,' she told each one.

At long last all the practising was over and it was time for the Nativity play to be presented.

On the Sunday night before Christmas, the children gathered excitedly in the church hall to put on their costumes for the play. Anna-Magdalena's mum was helping the shepherds get dressed up. They wore striped towelling robes with holes cut out for their arms. She wound a different-coloured cloth around each child's head.

Anna-Magdalena laughed when she saw Neville. Neville laughed when he saw Anna-Magdalena.

Then she saw Jack being helped into his costume. He had a purple cloak that went all the way to his feet and the most beautiful crown, the one that was glittery. His gift for the baby Jesus was a gold box with a sparkling top.

That's the best costume of all, thought Anna-Magdalena. Maybe next year it will be *my* turn to wear a crown, she said to herself. She took a deep breath and went over to Jack and said that she liked his costume.

He grinned happily and said he liked her shepherd's clothes too. Together they looked at and admired all the other children's costumes.

Then they noticed three of the grown-ups talking worriedly together.

'Sarah's got flu, and won't be coming tonight. Her mother just phoned,' said one of the grown-ups.

'Who will play the part of the angel?' said another.

'The only one who knows the words is Anna-Magdalena,' said Mrs Lander.

And so it happened that Anna-Magdalena was not a shepherd after all. Off came the coloured cloth from her head. Off came the striped robe. Off came the dark blue T-shirt under the robe.

Instead, Anna-Magdalena put on a long, white robe made from a sheet and tied at the waist with a narrow silver cord. Pinned to her back were two glittering silver wings. On her head went a silver circle with long silver points fanning out around her head like beams of light.

It was the most beautiful crown Anna-Magdalena had ever seen. It was called a halo.

The church was decorated with evergreen branches and lighted candles and was packed with people who had come to see the play.

Anna-Magdalena stood on a box so that everyone could see her. She held out her hands to greet Mary and to tell her she was going to have a very special baby.

Later, Anna-Magdalena held out her hands again and told the shepherds the exciting news of baby Jesus' birth.

Anna-Magdalena's halo shone in the candlelight and her glittering wings caught points of coloured light from the Christmas tree.

Anna-Magdalena stood very, very still, but she smiled and smiled. She knew that she was the happiest girl in the whole world.

ANNA-MAGDALENA GOES HEAD OVER HEELS

For Andrew Kinnear

Anna-Magdalena goes head over heels

Kay Kinnear

Illustrations by
Maureen Bradley

Contents

1

Anna-Magdalena's Dark Secret

Anna-Magdalena was a small person with blue eyes and orange hair. She had a straight fringe that she blew off her forehead whenever she was worried or cross. More often than not, her face wore a determined 'I-know-what-I-know' expression.

One of the things that Anna-Magdalena knew was that she loved her big, long name, all of it. But her family simply wouldn't use it. Mum and her stepdad, Gerald, called her Mags. So did Aunty Cath. Her Uncle Henry was even more hopeless. He called her Sausage. Worst of all, though she loved him dearly, was her Uncle Andy. He had orange hair just like hers and he was always calling her by different names. It could be Mags. It could be Maggy-Waggy, even Anna-Banana. It was very discouraging.

Last year, though, Anna-Magdalena had outsmarted her family. When Mum had a new baby, Anna-Magdalena had picked out his name. She chose Luke. It was a name so short that even *her* family couldn't find silly things to do with it. Baby Luke was crawling now and Anna-Magdalena often told him, 'I'll teach you to say my name right.'

So far, all he could say was, 'durdle, durdle, durdle.'

Anna-Magdalena never gave up on things easily. She was also quite a brave little girl. She liked the highest slide at the park. She wasn't afraid of water, even though she'd had to try and try before she learned to swim. She wasn't even afraid of spiders now.

But there *was* one thing Anna-Magdalena was frightened of. She was afraid of the dark. She hadn't told anybody. It was a secret.

In fact, it was such a secret that Anna-Magdalena hadn't known it herself until just this week when she broke the little nightlight on her bedside table. The light gave a friendly glow whenever she woke in the dark.

But two days ago, Anna-Magdalena had bounced into bed with her arms stretched out pretending to be a plane. Her right arm (or rather her right wing) clipped the lamp and sent it flying, and it fell on on the hard wooden floor and broke.

Mum sighed and picked up the broken pieces. Then Anna-Magdalena said her bedtime prayers. She asked God to bless everyone in her family. She said 'God bless Mummy and Gerald and Luke. God bless Aunty Cath and Uncle Henry. God bless Uncle Andy. And God bless me.'

'And help make you more careful,' added Mum.

'And help make me more careful,' prayed Anna-Magdalena. Being careful was not one of her strong points.

She snuggled down in her bed and went to sleep before her Uncle Andy could have said 'Anna-Banana' five times.

Several hours later, Anna-Magdalena woke up. The room was completely black. There was no friendly glow from her bedside lamp. She didn't know where she was and suddenly she felt afraid. She reached out her hand and it bumped into her teddy, who was called Bear.

She hugged Bear to her chest and slid further down into the bed. She whispered to herself, that in a moment or two, when she and Bear were feeling braver, they would go and ask Mum to turn on the landing light.

A few moments later, and before Bear had enough courage to get out of bed, Anna-Magdalena had fallen asleep again.

In the morning the sun streamed in through the window and Anna-Magdalena's bedroom looked the friendliest place in the world. She dragged Bear out from the very bottom of the bed where he had hidden.

'You were silly last night.' Anna-Magdalena said to the furry face and gave him a little shake. And then she forgot all about the darkness of the night.

Until bedtime. After her prayers, Anna-Magdalena said to her mum, 'I miss my light.'

Mum nodded. 'I'll get a new one next time I go shopping. Meanwhile I'll turn on the landing light. It'll shine into your room.'

In the middle of the night Anna-Magdalena had a bad dream. In the dream something she couldn't see very well was chasing her. She tried to run, but her legs wouldn't move. She shouted in her sleep and woke up.

The landing light *wasn't* on! The room was totally dark and Anna-Magdalena started to cry. She heard footsteps. The bedroom light came on and Anna-Magdalena was gathered into her mum's arms.

'Mags, I'm so sorry. Without thinking, I switched off the landing light when I went to bed.'

'You said you'd leave it on!' sobbed Anna-Magdalena, accusingly.

Mum squeezed her tight. 'I'm really sorry. Sometimes *mums* need to be more careful too. We'll pray for that tomorrow night.'

Anna-Magdalena wrapped her arms tightly round her mum, wanting to keep her sitting on the bed. Mum kissed her forehead and said, 'When you feel frightened, don't forget that God loves you. He's looking after you at night, as well as in the day.'

Anna-Magdalena nodded but now her eyelids felt very heavy. She lay back in her bed and was soon fast asleep.

Early the next evening Anna-Magdalena was playing ball with Patch, her tortoiseshell kitten. She had an orange patch on her head which was how she had got

her name. Mum had just gone into the kitchen to cook the tea.

Suddenly all the lights went out!

Gerald, Anna-Magdalena's stepdad, was upstairs, putting Luke to bed. He shouted, 'It must be a powercut!'

Anna-Magdalena's room was totally dark once more. She blew upon her fringe in a worried way. Her voice quavered as she called out to Gerald, 'Wh-where are you?'

'I'm here on the landing, walking towards you. Follow my voice,' he replied.

It wasn't nearly so bad with a voice to walk towards. Feeling her way around the bed and the door frame, Anna-Magdalena met Gerald on the landing. He took her hand.

'What's a power cut?' she asked. She felt perfectly safe now.

Gerald explained, 'It means there's no electricity. Something goes wrong at the power station where they make the electricity and the lights go out and all electrical machines like cookers and fridges stop running.'

They felt their way down the stairs and to the front door. They looked out. The whole street was black. No street lights, no lights at any of the windows.

'What we need are some candles,' said Gerald. 'Pauline, where are the candles?' he called out into the darkness to Anna-Magdalena's mum.

'Aren't they by the fuse-box in the cellar?' she

shouted from the kitchen. No, they weren't there.

'How about the sideboard?' she suggested next.

Gerald and Anna-Magdalena felt through the drawers. No, they weren't there.

Suddenly, it was as if a light went on in Anna-Magdalena's head. *She* remembered where the candles were.

'I know!' she exclaimed. In her excitement she forgot her fear of the dark. She left the safety of Gerald's side and felt her way round the sofa. Then she bumped into the table.

'Ouch!' she muttered. Anna-Magdalena felt round the table and into the hall downstairs. She opened the hall corner cupboard. There, on the bottom shelf, her fingers discovered a big box of candles.

'I've got the candles!' cried Anna-Magdalena. Back from the hall she came, carrying the box and feeling her way. She bumped into the table again and mumbled 'Ouch', even though this time it didn't hurt. Patting with her free hand round the sofa, she got back to Gerald.

'I saw the candles before,' explained Anna-Magdalena. 'Patch chased her ball into the cupboard. The door was open.'

'Well done!' said Gerald, scooping her up and giving her a big hug.

'That was brave of you,' said Mum, who'd come in from the kitchen. She kissed Anna-Magdalena.

Mum lit a candle and the first thing she saw was Anna-Magdalena's big, pleased grin.

After that, Gerald and Mum lit lots of candles and stood them in holders all round the sitting-room. It looked lovely, all glowing and friendly. Gerald lit the coal fire and soon the fireplace was full of friendly flames.

'We've got light. We'll soon have more heat,' said Gerald with satisfaction. 'Now, what about our tea?'

'I'm hungry,' Anna-Magdalena said. Suddenly she felt very hungry indeed.

Mum said, 'The cooker's electric, so that's useless. But I'll see what I can find.' She took two candles with her into the kitchen. In a little while, she returned carrying a tray. On it were uncooked sausages, slices of bread, margarine, ketchup, tomatoes, crisps, jam, apples, chocolate biscuits and apple juice.

Gerald found a pocket torch and went out of the kitchen door. In a moment he was back with two green sticks he'd cut from the shrub outside. Using a penknife, he whittled a pointy end to each stick and handed one to Anna-Magdalena.

He showed her how to thread a sausage on to her stick. 'Now hold it over the fire,' he said.

Mum toasted bread on a toasting fork while Gerald and Anna-Magdalena did the sausages.

'Done yet?' Anna-Magdalena asked, inspecting her blackening sausage.

'Probably not,' said Gerald. 'Don't hold it so near the flames. Give the inside of the sausage time to cook too.'

By the time Gerald declared the sausages finished,

Anna-Magdalena felt cooked herself, sitting there in front of the warm fire.

They ate sausages in toast with drippy ketchup, and then had tomatoes and crisps. The sausages tasted slightly burnt, but Anna-Magdalena was so hungry she didn't care. After that they drank juice and munched toast and jam, apples and chocolate biscuits. It was a really lovely picnic.

Anna-Magdalena glanced round the softly lit room. She thought it had never looked so nice. It was really cosy to have her mum and Gerald sitting on cushions beside her on the floor by the fire. 'Can we have tea like this tomorrow night?' she asked.

They laughed and promised that they would do it again the very next time there was a powercut.

'I hope the lights go out soon,' said Anna-Magdalena. She thought for a moment. "Cept in my room,' she added.

Next day they went to the shops. Anna-Magdalena chose a wonderful new night lamp. It was a china teddybear in a pink china nightie and nightcap. The teddy was open at the back and held a little bulb. The light shone through holes round the neckline and hem of the teddy's nightie. Mum put it on a high shelf in the bedroom for safety.

Anna-Magdalena thought it was the best lamp she'd ever seen. And Bear promised not to be jealous of the new teddy.

2

Anna-Magdalena
asks Why? Why? Why?

One winter morning Anna-Magdalena was helping her mum move Sam's cage from the kitchen out into the garden. Sam was Anna-Magdalena's guinea-pig and normally he stayed in the shed at night. But last night's weather forecast had said it would be very cold, well below freezing, so they had brought Sam inside.

It was cold today too and Anna-Magdalena was all bundled up. She wore a warm jacket and a woolly hat, scarf and mittens. She and her mum set the cage down in the sunshine. Anna-Magdalena went back into the kitchen to collect Sam's food. He had spinach greens, lettuce and pieces of apple and carrot.

Spinach was Sam's favourite food. Not that he said so, of course. But Anna-Magdalena had noticed that he always ate it first.

'Why does Sam like spinach best?' asked Anna-Magdalena. 'I think it's horrible.'

'I don't know,' replied her mum. Mum could usually

answer Anna-Magdalena's questions but not absolutely always.

Anna-Magdalena moved round to the side of the cage. She checked to see if Sam showed any signs of growing a tail. No, no tail. Mum had said that guinea-pigs didn't have tails, but Anna-Magdalena kept hoping. She thought Sam would look lovely with a tail. She asked her mum, not for the first time, 'Why don't guinea-pigs get tails? Tell me again, I've forgotten.'

Mum said, 'Animals have the bodies they need. Cats use their tails for balance when they jump. Horses brush off flies with theirs. Guinea-pigs lead a quiet life and so they don't need tails.'

Anna-Magdalena said 'Oh,' and went to find her bike in the garden shed. She rode twice round the garden. The second time she stopped at the gap in the hedge between her house and their neighbour, Granny Charles. The old lady was sitting by the window and Anna-Magdalena waved.

Granny Charles wasn't Anna-Magdalena's real granny, but she *was* a very special friend. And Granny Charles was always very kind to Anna-Magdalena.

She often invited Anna-Magdalena inside for milk and a biscuit or to hear a story. At the very least she would open the window and they would have a chat. But today it was too cold for an open window. Granny Charles waved and folded her arms across her chest and pretended to shiver.

Anna-Magdalena wrapped her arms across her chest

and pretended to shiver too. She would have liked to ask Granny why it was so cold. Granny pointed at the book on the table, which meant, Anna-Magdalena knew, that she was in the middle of her reading.

Every day Granny Charles read her Bible and sometimes she told Anna-Magdalena interesting stories from it. Anna-Magdalena's favourite was the one where Jesus walked on water.

'Why could he do that?' she wanted to know.

'Because he was God's Son and could do anything,' Granny had answered. Granny Charles always answered all of Anna-Magdalena's questions. She also called her small friend by her full name, Anna-Magdalena, not Maggy-Waggy or anything funny. Granny was a great friend to have.

But now the old lady returned to her reading and Anna-Magdalena went back to riding around the garden. It certainly was a cold day. She really began to shiver, so she decided to put the bike back into the shed and go indoors.

Suddenly she noticed that the shed window had icy patterns on it. They were beautiful, like trees and leaves, only in white frost. Anna-Magdalena hadn't seen that on any window before.

Back inside the kitchen, she took off her outdoor clothes and told her mum about the icy pictures.

'What are they?' asked Anna-Magdalena.

Mum answered, 'Well, the air all around us carries some water in it. It can carry more water when it's warm than when it's cold. It got so cold last night that the air had to get rid of some of its water, so it left it as frost on the windows.'

'Why do they look like trees?' asked Anna-Magdalena.

'Ummm,' said her mum. 'That's a hard question. I could say that it's one of the beautiful designs that God has made for our world...'

She paused while she hung up Anna-Magdalena's jacket in the coat cupboard. Then she went on, 'I don't understand *how* it works exactly. The patterns form when the wetness in the air goes straight to frost on the windows without ever being water in between—I think.' She smiled at her daughter's puzzled face. 'You don't understand, do you?'

'Yes, I do!' said Anna-Magdalena, even though she didn't. She always preferred to be told too much rather than too little.

At that moment, Patch, Anna-Magdalena's kitten, scurried in from the sitting- room. She circled round their legs, wanting to play ball. Anna-Magdalena picked up the kitten and tickled it behind the ear. Then she said, 'It's so cold. Can I put another blanket in Patch's basket?'

'Good idea,' said Mum.

Anna-Magdalena rummaged through her mum's bag of spare material. She found one soft blue cloth and one soft red cloth about the same size.

'Which colour will Patch like? Red or blue?' Anna-Magdalena asked her mum.

113

To her surprise, Mum answered, 'Cats don't see colours. So choose the one *you* like best.'

Cats don't see colours! Anna-Magdalena was horrified. *Poor Patch!*

'Why not?' she demanded.

Her mum replied, 'They don't need to know colours. They need to see at night instead.'

'How?' asked Anna-Magdalena. She didn't feel quite so sorry for Patch now.

'Look at Patch's eyes. See the black part in the middle? Those are called the pupils.'

Anna-Magdalena peered into Patch's furry face. The black parts in the centre of her green eyes were thin slits. Her mum looked too.

She said, 'Those slits open up really big and wide at night to bring in more light. Also there are mirror bits at the back of her eyes to get as much light as possible.'

'Why?' asked Anna-Magdalena.

'Cats hunt at night for food. So they need to see better.'

Anna-Magdalena stared into Patch's eyes to see if she could see the mirrors. But Patch was fed up with all this attention. She wriggled free and jumped to the floor.

'Why . . . ?' began Anna-Magdalena.

But Mum shooed her into the sitting-room saying, 'No more questions for a minute. I want to wash the kitchen floor. Ask Luke if he'd like you to play with him.'

Anna-Magdalena protested, 'But he won't answer.' It was no good asking *him* things.

Luke was in his playpen. He bobbed up and down with delight when he saw Anna-Magdalena. Luke was her number one fan. While he watched, Anna-Magdalena put her head down on the carpet and stuck one leg in the air. She was trying to learn to stand on her head. This was as far as she had got, however. Each time she tried, the second leg simply refused to come off the floor.

Anna-Magdalena stood up again and clambered over the top of Luke's playpen. She sat down beside him and piled up a tower of green and yellow bricks. He knocked them over happily. It was a game they had played a lot. He said, 'Durdle,' and gave her a huge toothless grin.

Only, was it toothless? There was a white spot in the bottom of his mouth. Anna-Magdalena stared into his jolly face with all the attention she had just given Patch.

Suddenly she cried, 'Mummy! Come and look at Luke!'

The swish, swish of a mop could be heard. 'In a minute,' called her mum.

Anna-Magdalena crawled back over the top of the playpen and ran to the door of the kitchen.

'Stop! Don't walk on the wet floor,' her mum ordered.

'Luke's got a little tooth. Come and see,' shouted Anna-Magdalena in her excitement.

This was real news! Luke was late getting his first tooth. She'd heard her mum and Gerald talking about it. Now Mum hurried into the sitting-room and scooped up the baby. He grinned again, proudly showing his new starter tooth.

'Why is it so small?' asked Anna-Magdalena.

Mum answered, 'It's not all the way through yet.'

'Where are his other teeth?'

Mum pointed to the two pink ridges in the baby's mouth. She said, 'They're all here in his gums.'

'How many teeth?' asked Anna-Magdalena.

'Same as you,' Mum smiled. 'Can you count?'

Anna-Magdalena trailed a finger along her bottom row of teeth, counting as she went. Then she did the top row.

'Nineteen!' she cried.

'That can't be right,' said Mum, laughing. 'Let's count again. You feel and count and I'll look and count. We'll see if we get the same answer.' Luke, who was tucked under his mum's arm, gazed into his sister's mouth too.

This time they both counted 'twenty' so they knew that must be the right number. As she put Luke back into the playpen, Mum said to Anna-Magdalena, 'Of course, *you'll* start losing *your* teeth about this time next year.'

Anna-Magdalena's jaw dropped, showing nearly all her twenty nice, white teeth. She thought how awful she'd look without teeth. She blew the orange fringe off her forehead in a worried way. What would she eat? Soup! She scowled at the thought of only eating soup. No chocolate biscuits.

Mum burst out laughing. 'Don't look so worried. You don't lose your teeth all at once.' She sat down and pulled Anna-Magdalena onto her lap. 'Anyway, as the old ones fall out, the new ones start to come in. New, bigger, stronger teeth.'

'Why ...?' started Anna-Magdalena.

'Why two sets of teeth?' This time Mum knew what the question would be. 'Baby teeth fit a little child's size. But they'd be much too small for an older child or grown-up.'

Mum smiled. 'It would be like Gerald wearing Luke's cap. It would sit like a cherry on top of his head.'

Anna-Magdalena giggled. That would be really silly. Mum gave her a big hug, lifted her off her lap, and stood up. She added, 'After all, when God made the world he had everything well planned. Sometimes people mess it up, but natural things usually work well. Now, absolutely no more questions. I've got work to do.'

But today Anna-Magdalena was unstoppable. The whys and whens and wheres and hows continued to come, thick and fast. There was just so *much* Anna-Magdalena wanted to know. Mum's work got further and further behind.

Finally, in despair, she poured her daughter a glass of milk and got out a big, sticky, iced bun. Surely there would be a few moments of quiet while Anna Magdalena's mouth was busy with the bun.

It worked! The bun was delicious and Anna-Magdalena chewed her first bite thoughtfully. And silently! She picked the raisins off the top and put them on her plate. Before she took each bite, she checked for raisins. Every single one was removed and placed on her plate.

Anna-Magdalena hated raisins. She thought they looked like little beetles. She arranged them in two rows across her plate.

By now, Anna-Magdalena had been quiet for a full five minutes. Eating her bun and drinking her milk had taken a lot of concentration. At last she took a huge breath and said in a rush, 'Mummy-where-do-raisins come-from?-Do-they-grow-on-trees?-They're-wrinkly. Are-they-old?-Why-can't-Luke-eat-raisins?-Can-I-have another-bun?-Why-not?'

3

Anna-Magdalena
and the Easter Eggs

It was the Saturday afternoon before Easter and Anna-Magdalena and her mum were going to do something exciting. They were going to colour eggs for a table decoration for Easter Sunday.

Mum took a dozen small eggs from an eggbox. She carefully lowered ten eggs into a big pan, added cold water and put them on the cooker to boil. The other two eggs she set aside in a small pan with water.

Anna-Magdalena, who was wearing a plastic apron, knelt on a chair at the kitchen table. Mum handed her an onion. It had cuts in its brown skin. Mum showed Anna-Magdalena how to pull off the pieces of brown, papery onion skin, layer by layer, until the onion was gleaming and white.

'Pooh, my fingers smell,' said Anna-Magdalena as she gave her mum the pieces of onion skin. 'What do you want them for?' she asked curiously.

'Wait and see,' said Mum. 'It's a surprise.'

The pieces of onion skin went into the small pan with the two eggs. Then Mum put it on the cooker to boil.

She covered the kitchen table with layers of newspaper. Then she got out three little bottles of food colouring and three cups. 'Pour a few drops into each cup,' she said. Very carefully, Anna-Magdalena dripped red food colouring into one cup, blue into another cup, and green into the third.

Now she had red, blue and green fingers which smelled of onions. Anna-Magdalena pulled a chair to the kitchen sink and stood on it to wash her hands.

After a while the eggs were ready and Mum took the pans off the cooker and emptied the hot water into the sink. 'What do you think of this?' Mum asked, showing Anna-Magdalena the two eggs in the small pan. They were bright yellow!

'How did they get yellow?' Anna-Magdalena demanded in surprise.

'The yellow comes from the onion skin you peeled,' said Mum smiling. 'Now we'll colour the other eggs.'

Mum poured water from the kettle into each cup with the drops of food colouring. Now, one cup had red water, one had blue water and the other green water. Mum gave Anna-Magdalena a big spoon and put the pan of plain boiled eggs on the table. Although there was no water in the pan, the eggs were still very hot.

'Choose an egg and gently put it into the colour you want,' instructed Mum. 'Be careful, the water's still hot.'

'Red!' cried Anna-Magdalena, scooping up an egg

121

with the big spoon. She dropped her egg into the red cup. There was a cracking noise and red water splashed over the sides of the cup onto the newspaper.

'Oh!' said Anna-Magdalena, peering into the cup. 'It's cracked.'

'Gently does it,' said Mum. 'They look prettier if they're not cracked.' She carefully slid an egg into the blue cup. 'Now we'll wait a few minutes.'

'A long time ago,' said Mum, 'Easter Sunday was known as Egg Sunday.'

'Why?' asked Anna-Magdalena as she turned her egg over in the cup with her big spoon.

'People brought beautifully coloured boiled eggs like these to the church and the priest blessed them. Then they gave the eggs away for gifts. They were to remind people about new life.'

'My egg's *pink*,' declared Anna-Magdalena.

'They won't dye really strong red or blue or green, just nice pale colours. Yours is done, I think,' said Mum.

So Anna-Magdalena scooped out her pink egg and put it into the eggbox to dry. The egg had a large crack, but when she turned it over the crack didn't show at all.

Next Anna-Magdalena dyed a blue egg and then a green one. 'I've done all the colours,' she said, feeling very pleased with her work.

'Make a purple egg,' suggested Mum.

Anna-Magdalena looked puzzled, 'But there's no purple cup,' she said, looking at the three cups.

'Put it in the red and afterwards in the blue,' said Mum. 'Those two colours make purple.'

Sure enough, using the red dye and the blue dye, Anna-Magdalena made a purple egg. Then she created a beautiful blue-green egg.

'Now I'm going to make a red, blue and green egg,' she announced. 'That will be the best of all.'

'Hmmm . . . we'll see,' said Mum.

Biting her lip, Anna-Magdalena concentrated very hard. She couldn't wait to inspect her most beautiful egg. First she put it in red, then in blue. It was a lovely purple. Then she lowered it into the green. When she spooned it up, it was a horrible sight! Sort of browny, sludgy, purply grey, the colour plasticine goes when it gets all muddled together.

'Ugh!' said Anna-Magdalena.

'Never mind,' said Mum. 'It was interesting to try. It's the red and green that don't go together prettily.'

Mum brought the last three eggs to the table. She said 'There *is* one way to use all the colours.' She put several drops of vegetable oil into each cup. 'We'll make eggs that are marbled. They can be two or three colours at once but they stay more separate.'

Mum showed Anna-Magdalena how to hold the egg so that only part of it went into the colour. 'The oil keeps it from getting coloured everywhere,' she said.

Anna-Magdalena put her egg into each colour in turn and it became the most wonderful collection of shades. Some spotty places it was just plain egg-coloured. Some places it was just pink, some just blue. Then it was patched with purple and blue-green. And finally a little bit of sludgy grey, but not enough to spoil it.

Anna-Magdalena was delighted and made two more marbled eggs, each one completely different and pretty.

'They're the best,' decided Anna-Magdalena. She looked down at her hands. She was marbled and multi-coloured and oily, too, right up to her elbows.

Mum pulled a chair to the sink again and gave her a bar of soap. Anna Magdalena scrubbed away and Mum wiped her face before pronouncing her more or less clean. When Mum had cleared away the splashed newspaper, the cups and the spoons, they sat down at the table with a glass of orange juice and a chocolate biscuit each.

Anna-Magdalena looked with satisfaction at the beautiful selection of coloured eggs drying in the eggbox.

Mum looked at the eggs, too. 'We always made coloured eggs when I was a little girl. It's a nice thing to do at Easter. But you know what Easter's really about, don't you?'

'It's about Jesus, not bunnies and chocolate eggs,' said Anna-Magdalena promptly. She had heard this last week at Sunday school.

'That's right,' said Mum. 'And did you find out something about Jesus in Sunday school?'

Anna-Magdalena thought for a moment. 'We had hot cross buns, ' she remembered.

Mum laughed. 'Trust you to remember the food best. The hot cross buns are to remind us that Jesus died on the cross for us.'

'Oh yes,' Anna-Magdalena remembered it all now. 'Jesus' friends were sad. They thought he was dead.'

'He *was* dead,' said Mum. 'But they didn't have to be sad for long,' she continued. 'Because three days later on Easter Sunday, Jesus was alive again.'

'And his friends all saw him,' said Anna-Magdalena. 'They were happy again.'

Anna-Magdalena finished her juice and biscuit and took off her apron.

'The eggs are dry,' said Mum. 'Would you like to take one of the best eggs to Granny Charles? And how about taking one to the new little boy who's moved in down the road?'

Anna-Magdalena's face took on a stubborn look. She blew the orange fringe off her forehead. 'We *need* our eggs for our table,' she said firmly.

'I'm going to put spring flowers with the eggs,' said Mum. 'I'm sure ten eggs will be enough to make a lovely decoration.'

Anna-Magdalena thought about Granny Charles, her special friend who lived next door. She changed her mind. 'I will take a marble egg to Granny.'

'Good,' said her mum. 'And the little boy?'

Anna-Magdalena couldn't bear the thought of giving away two of the beautiful marble eggs. She'd seen the boy yesterday and he'd stuck out his tongue. Why should she give him an egg? 'He stuck out his tongue at me,' she explained to her mum.

'It doesn't matter,' said Mum, shaking her head. 'It would be a way to make friends.'

Anna-Magdalena gave in. 'He can have the pink egg—the first one I did,' she said.

'No, he can't!' said Mum, frowning. 'That one's cracked.'

Sometimes Mum could be as determined as Anna-Magdalena. 'Remember how the people in the old days gave *nice* eggs as gifts? We're going to do that too. If you won't take him a beautiful egg, *I* will.'

As she said this, Mum packed two marbled eggs with tissue paper in two little boxes. In one of the boxes, she tucked a small packet of chocolate drops.

Anna-Magdalena's eyes glinted at the sight of the chocolate drops. It wasn't fair. The sticking-out-tongue-boy was going to get sweets, too.

Anna-Magdalena's face looked like a thundercloud as she took the first box and marched crossly down the street. Her mum stood on the front steps to watch. At the boy's house, Anna-Magdalena reached up and rang the bell. Almost at once the door opened and the sticking-out-tongue-boy stood in front of her.

'H'lo' he said.

'H'lo,' said Anna-Magdalena. 'Here's an egg,' she said rather rudely, pushing the egg towards him.

To her surprise, the boy's face totally changed. He broke into a huge, sunny smile. 'For me?' he asked. 'Look

Mum!' His mum had appeared behind him and she smiled at Anna-Magdalena.

'What a nice Easter surprise,' she said. 'Thank you.'

'I'm getting a puppy tomorrow,' said the boy. 'D'you want to see him?'

A puppy! Anna-Magdalena's face lit up in a smile to match the boy's.

The boy's mother leaned forward out of the door and waved at Anna-Magdalena's mum. She said to her visitor, 'I'll arrange with your mother for you to come and play early next week, if you'd like to see the puppy.'

'Oh yes,' said Anna-Magdalena. 'Bye,' she said to the boy. 'See you.'

'See you,' he replied and grinned.

'He didn't stick his tongue out once,' Anna-Magdalena informed her mum when she got home. 'He's getting a puppy and I can play with it.'

'That's great,' said Mum and patted her on the shoulder. Then she handed her Granny's eggbox.

Anna-Magdalena went round the house and popped through the gap in the hedge. She knocked on Granny's back door.

Granny Charles' face, too, took on a big smile when she saw Anna-Magdalena and the box. 'What a beautiful egg!' she said admiringly. 'I've never seen one with so many colours.'

Granny had been baking biscuits in her kitchen. She asked Anna-Magdalena to come in and sample one to see if they were up to standard.

Anna-Magdalena tested her biscuit by putting the whole thing in her mouth at once. When she was able to speak again, she said it was yummy. Then she told Granny how to make marbled Easter eggs.

When it was time for Anna-Magdalena to go home, Granny said, 'I have something for you too.' And she gave Anna-Magdalena a box with a shiny red bow on top. Inside was a huge delicious-looking chocolate egg.

After thanking Granny and giving her a hug, Anna-Magdalena raced home to show her present.

'Giving away eggs *is* a good idea,' she told her mum. She was glad they'd thought of it.

4

Anna-Magdalena
Digs a Pond

Anna-Magdalena, her stepdad Gerald and her Uncle Andy were standing in the back garden staring at a patch of grass. In their imagination they were seeing a pond. A lovely pond with clear water and frogs and tadpoles and fish and flowers round the edge. Anna-Magdalena and Gerald had seen a pond like that at a friend's house, and now they were going to make one in their garden.

Gerald got out a metal tape and began to measure. Uncle Andy asked, 'What shape do you want? Round, oval, square, blob-shaped, kidney?'

'What's kidney?' asked Anna-Magdalena, looking up at Uncle Andy, one of her very favourite grown-ups. He had orange hair just like hers and lots and lots of freckles.

'Kidney?' repeated Uncle Andy. For an answer he drew a shape in the air with his hand.

'That's a bean!' shouted Anna-Magdalena.

'A bean. Exactly,' said Gerald, who glanced up from his measuring.

'Who's for a bean, then?' demanded Uncle Andy. 'Raise your right hand.'

Four hands went up. Anna-Magdalena raised both hands because she had forgotten which was her right side.

'Four votes from three people for the bean,' said Uncle Andy. 'That has to be the winner.'

They got the garden hose out of the shed. While Anna-Magdalena stood on one end of the hose, Gerald and Uncle Andy curled it round in the shape of a bean. Then the three of them stood back to look at it.

'Pop in and get your mum, Mags,' said Gerald. 'Let's see what she thinks.'

Mum was doing some work at the kitchen table. But she left the big books with lines and numbers in them and came out into the garden.

'Brilliant!' she said at once. 'I like the shape and size. When I finish my accounts, I'll come out and help.'

Uncle Andy and Gerald dug round the edge of the hose to get the shape of the pond and then they took the hose away. Now the diggers set to work in earnest. Uncle Andy loosened the soil at one end of the bean with a garden fork and Anna-Magdalena began to dig there with her small spade. The two men began at the other end with big shovels.

While the men dug steadily, Anna-Magdalena sometimes dug, sometimes did other things. When she had scooped a hole the size of a washing-up bowl, she thought it was time to practise standing on her head.

She pressed her forehead to the grass and lifted one leg in the air. She still couldn't do it! The other leg just didn't want to go up.

'Oh, look,' cried Uncle Andy. 'Anna-Banana is trying out an upside-down view of the bean.'

She grinned and managed to lift the other leg a little bit. Then she tumbled over. She dug some more. When she had dug a really big hole, she went into the house. She came out with a plastic container of water and poured the water into the hole and began to make mud pies.

Uncle Andy came to inspect. 'One of our labourers here has started to fill her end of the pond,' he said to Gerald.

'I'm making chocolate pies for your tea,' said Anna-Magdalena, waggling fingers at him that looked like black sausages.

'I'm looking forward to that,' said Uncle Andy and clutched his throat and made being-sick sounds.

Anna-Magdalena giggled.

After a while, Mum came out with a tea tray for the workers. She took Anna-Magdalena over to the outside tap and washed the mud off her hands and arms. The three diggers ate biscuits and drank tea. Anna-Magdalena didn't actually like tea very much, but sometimes she pretended she did to be grown up.

Meanwhile, Mum picked up one of the shovels. She did some digging while the other three watched. After fifteen minutes, she went back to her bookwork and the main digging team began again.

Towards the end of the afternoon the big hole dug by Uncle Andy, Gerald and Mum joined up with the small hole dug by Anna-Magdalena. The digging was finished.

Anna-Magdalena inspected the work. Along the long sides of the bean were two ledges. 'What are the steps for?' she asked.

'Some plants and animals like deep water, others like shallow water,' Gerald explained. 'Look, we've made a shallow step here so that the fish can lay their eggs.'

'We can probably finish the pond tomorrow,' Gerald said to Uncle Andy. Anna-Magdalena smiled happily. By tomorrow, she thought to herself, her pond would be full of animals and fish.

The next day, the edges of the pond were levelled and sand was poured into the bottom. And then it was time to get the hose out again. Anna-Magdalena hoped they were going to fill it up.

The hose was turned on. But it wasn't to fill the pond. Uncle Andy started to wet piles of newspaper and stick them on the sloping sides of the pond to hold the earth in place. Anna-Magdalena was bored. Why was it all taking so long?

'Would you like to help?' asked Uncle Andy, handing her the hose. Suddenly, the temptation was too great. Anna-Magdalena put her thumb partly over the end of the hose, and the water came whooshing out. She sprayed Uncle Andy right in the back of his neck.

Uncle Andy gave a great roar. Anna-Magdalena squealed, dropped the hose and ran away giggling and screaming. Uncle Andy picked up the hose and with his long legs soon caught her. Anna-Magdalena shrieked and giggled at the same time. Now they were both wet.

Hearing the commotion, Mum brought out a big bath towel and some dry clothes for Anna-Magdalena. As they dried off, Uncle Andy said, 'Tell you what. I won't spray you if you don't spray me.'

'OK,' said Anna-Magdalena.

'Promise?'

'Promise,' said Anna-Magdalena. 'But when's it going to be a pond?'

'Just you watch,' said Gerald, unrolling a huge sheet of thick, blue plastic. He and Uncle Andy pulled it over the hole and then pressed it down into the hole. Then they put bricks and stones round the edges of the plastic to hold it firm.

'This is the lining,' said Gerald. 'If we didn't line the hole with plastic, then all the water would run away. And now,' he said, 'we can fill it.'

Uncle Andy handed the hose to Anna-Magdalena. 'Promise?' he asked again.

'Promise,' said Anna-Magdalena. This really was the best bit of all. She held the hose and filled the pond with water while the two grown-ups straightened and stretched the plastic and sometimes moved the stones. This was so the plastic lining would fit tightly against the hole.

At last the pond was full of water. Gerald trimmed off the ends of the plastic while Mum, Anna-Magdalena and Uncle Andy arranged stones all around the edge of the pond.

The bean looked wonderful.

'Will the animals come tonight?' asked Anna-Magdalena.

'We have to give the pond time to settle in,' said Mum. 'Good things are worth waiting for. Anyway, we'll plant some plants this week.'

Gerald said to Anna-Magdalena in a serious voice, 'Next weekend we'll fence off the pond. So, just for this week you must only visit the pond with a grown-up. You must not come out here on your own. We don't want you falling in. Will you remember?'

Anna-Magdalena nodded. 'Yes,' she said. 'And I'll make sure Luke doesn't fall in either.'

'Good girl,' said Gerald.

The next day Mum, Anna-Magdalena and Luke went to the garden centre and bought some plants—feathery ferns, striped yellow and green long grass, iris flowers and a water-lily. When they got home Mum and Anna-Magdalena planted them and the pond started to look like a pond, especially with the water-lily pads floating on the surface. But there were no animals.

'Can we buy some fish?' Anna-Magdalena asked. 'The plants look lonely.'

'The water's not ready yet,' said Mum. 'If we put fish in too soon, they'll get mould on them. It's a sort of grey covering that makes them ill.'

Next morning Mum and Anna-Magdalena went out to look at the pond. 'When will the frogs come?' asked Anna-Magdalena. If there weren't any fish, there could at least be some frogs.

'It's too late to get frogs laying eggs here this year,' answered Mum, 'but I'm sure they'll find us soon.'

'Tomorrow?' asked Anna-Magdalena hopefully. What was the good of a pond without frogs or fish, she thought.

'I don't know when they'll come,' said Mum. 'Insects need to come first so the frogs have something to eat.'

Every morning Anna-Magdalena and her mum looked at the pond. The water-lilies looked fine but it wasn't much fun without animals. There were a few insects but that didn't really count.

'We *must* have frogs and fish,' said Anna-Magdalena in a small but determined voice. 'They've got to come *now*.'

'Be patient,' both grown-ups said, but Anna-Magdalena was tired of being patient.

Two weeks passed. Early one evening Gerald came home from work and said, 'Come out and look at the bean with me.'

'I'm making a picture,' said Anna-Magdalena who was lying on the carpet drawing. She hadn't bothered to look at the pond for several days.

'Come on, Mags,' said Gerald, holding out a hand. He pulled her up.

They went outside. The pond was fenced now with a gate. They unlocked the gate and at once Anna-Magdalena spotted something at the edge of the water.

'What's that? What's that?' she shouted, jumping up and down. She looked down into the water. There was a plastic bag holding water and five little goldfish.

'Why are they in a bag?' asked Anna-Magdalena.

'We're waiting until the water in the bag gets as cool as the water in the pond,' Gerald answered.

Anna-Magdalena looked puzzled.

Gerald explained, 'If the fish suddenly go from warmish water in the bag to cold pond water it could be too big a shock. They might die.'

'Oh.' Anna-Magdalena's eyes grew very large. She blew the orange fringe off her forehead. She didn't want her fish to die.

Later, Gerald opened the bag. The five goldfish swam out and began to flit around the pond.

'I think they like it,' cried Anna-Magdalena happily.

Gerald got a little tin out of his pocket. 'Here, you can feed them,' he said. 'Just a little, not too much.'

Anna-Magdalena scattered a few goldfish flakes on the surface of the pond. The little fish nosed up to the flakes and began to eat.

Anna-Magdalena clapped her hands with delight.

Next morning while Mum was hanging out washing Anna-Magdalena decided to name her fish. Big Goldie. Little Goldie. Spot (it had one white spot). Whitey (it had a white tail). Bumpy (it had a small bump on its head).

Anna-Magdalena was peering into the water trying to keep track of which fish was which when she caught sight of something.

A small nose stuck out of the water. And there, clinging to the side of the pond, was the first animal to find the pond by itself. It was a frog. It was near the stripey grass they'd planted. And when Anna-Magdalena looked carefully, she saw *another* frog sitting on the bank among the clumps of grass.

'Oh Mummy, Mummy, look!' she cried. 'My frogs have come!'

It had been worth waiting for. It was a real pond at last.

5

Anna-Magdalena
Starts a Fight

Anna-Magdalena put on a cardigan and said to her mum, 'I'm ready.' She was going to play at Ollie's house. The sticking-out-tongue-boy, she had discovered, was called Oliver, but he had said she must call him Ollie.

Anna-Magdalena had said she was called Anna-Magdalena, and he must call her that. But when Ollie said it, it came out like Anna Magda*wena*. After several tries they settled on Anna.

Anna-Magdalena reached up and rang the bell at his front door. She waved at her mum who was standing on their own front steps down the road.

The door opened. 'H'lo, Anna,' said the boy.

'H'lo, Ollie,' said Anna-Magdalena.

A little puppy was jumping up and down around his legs. It was a cocker spaniel with a shiny black coat and big brown eyes. Anna-Magdalena thought it was the most wonderful pet she'd ever seen, next to Patch, her own kitten, of course.

'What's his name?' she asked Ollie. The last time she'd been to his house the puppy had just arrived and hadn't got a name. On that day Ollie couldn't decide whether to call him Blackie or Spot.

Anna-Magdalena had pointed out that you couldn't call a dog Spot when he didn't have any spots. Ollie had said he could call his dog anything he wanted and he liked the name Spot. Luckily, Ollie's mum had arrived with orange juice and biscuits and they had forgotten the argument.

So today Anna-Magdalena was specially curious to know the puppy's name. 'He's called Flops,' Ollie said proudly. 'See! Because of his ears.'

The puppy did truly have floppy ears. They swung and flapped and flopped when he ran. Anna-Magdalena smiled. 'That's a good name,' she said admiringly. 'Much better than Spot.'

Ollie's face lost its happy smile. 'Spot's a good name, too,' he muttered stubbornly.

'But not when ...' Anna-Magdalena started to say.

She was interrupted by Ollie's mum who asked whether she'd like to try Ollie's new bowling game. 'The puppy loves playing it,' she added.

They went out into the back garden and set up the plastic skittles on the grass. 'Roll the ball at the skittles,' instructed Ollie. 'Try to knock them all down.'

Anna-Magdalena took the heavy blue plastic ball and rolled it. Flops chased the ball, trying to bite it. The ball knocked down four skittles. The jumping, scrambling, barking puppy pushed over the rest. It was a great success.

Ollie and Anna-Magdalena took turns. Almost every time with Flops' help they managed to knock down all the skittles.

After a while they sat down on the grass to decide what to do next. Anna-Magdalena stroked the puppy.

'He's got big paws,' said Ollie.

'That means he'll be a big dog,' said Anna-Magdalena. 'That's what big paws mean, my Uncle Andy says.'

Ollie looked at his trainers. He had quite big feet for his age. 'Does it work for people?' he asked.

'Of course,' Anna-Magdalena said confidently. Then she studied her own small sandals. She hoped it wasn't true, after all. But she didn't want to say she might have been wrong.

Ollie stood up and took a piece of chocolate from his pocket. 'Here, Flops,' he called. The little dog bounded forward wagging his tail.

'Don't give him chocolate,' ordered Anna-Magdalena. 'It's not good for dogs.'

'It *is*,' said Ollie.

'No, it's not good for dogs,' repeated Anna-Magdalena and tried to snatch the piece of chocolate from Ollie's hand.

'It *is*, it *is*,' Ollie shouted.

'It's *not*, it's *not*,' Anna-Magdalena shouted back. She was a small, determined person who liked to be right.

Ollie's face went red and he pushed Anna-Magdalena.

She stumbled backwards and her mouth dropped open in astonishment. She was *not* used to being pushed. Without thinking, she took a run at Ollie and pushed him hard. Her strength took Ollie by surprise and he staggered backwards and fell onto the grass. His arm caught the edge of the stone path and he began to cry.

Anna-Magdalena saw with alarm that his arm was bleeding. She blew the straight orange fringe off her forehead in a worried way. When Ollie, too, saw the big scrape on his elbow, he yelled harder and headed for the house.

His mum had heard the noise and was coming out to find them. 'What happened?' she asked.

'Anna pushed me and I fell,' said Ollie through his tears, glaring at Anna-Magdalena.

'He pushed me first,' Anna-Magdalena said, looking cross and worried at the same time.

They went into the house and Ollie's mum bathed his arm. She dabbed antiseptic on it to clean away the germs. 'Ow! Ow!' sobbed Ollie. The antiseptic stung. Anna-Magdalena was watching. She felt sorry he was hurt. But *he* pushed me first, she thought.

Then Ollie's mum put a big, square plaster on his arm. Finally, she wiped his face and gave him a tissue to blow his nose.

'Tell her to go home,' Ollie begged his mum, looking at Anna-Magdalena from behind her skirt.

Ollie's mum turned to Anna-Magdalena, 'His arm is probably quite sore and may be bruised. Perhaps it

144

would be a good idea for you to go home now. You can come to play another day.'

Ollie and Anna-Magdalena glared at one another. Both were thinking they never wanted to play together again. Anna-Magdalena marched out of Ollie's house and down the path while Ollie and his mum watched from the steps until she reached her own front door.

Stomp, stomp, stomp went Anna-Magdalena into her own house. She knew she was right about the chocolate, but she felt wrong, too. It was an odd feeling.

'You're back early,' said her mum. When she saw Anna-Magdalena's face she knew at once that something had happened.

'Ollie pushed me 'n' I pushed him back. He fell. He hurt his arm,' said Anna Magdalena crossly.

Mum asked more questions until she was sure that Ollie wasn't hurt badly. 'Let's talk about this,' she said. So they went into the sitting-room and sat on the sofa.

'Why did you push Ollie?' asked Mum.

'He pushed *me*,' Anna-Magdalena explained.

Mum nodded. 'I know, but that's not what we do, is it? What would Jesus like us to do when somebody does something unkind, like pushing?' Mum lifted Anna Magdalena onto her lap. 'Do we do something bad and unkind back?' she asked.

Anna-Magdalena's face was downcast. 'No,' she said. She knew it was wrong.

'What do we do then?' continued Mum, gently.

Anna-Magdalena thought and then said, 'We do something good.'

'That's right!' Mum smiled at Anna-Magdalena. 'So what could you have done when Ollie pushed you?'

Anna-Magdalena thought again. 'I could've said "Don't push—let's play."'

'Well done. That would have been much better,' Mum said approvingly. 'And you would still be at his house playing with the puppy instead of back home with nothing special to do.'

Anna-Magdalena's face looked really sorry. Mum gave her a hug. 'Don't look so sad. None of us is perfect. But Jesus loves us, even when we're bad.'

She slid Anna-Magdalena off her lap and stood up. 'You'll have to play on your own for a little while. Later on, before Luke wakes up from his nap, you can help me make a cake. But first I want to have a word with Ollie's mum.' She went to the phone, looked at a list, and pressed the buttons.

Anna-Magdalena went into the back garden and said 'hallo' to Sam, her guinea-pig. Then she went to count the frogs in the pond. She looked through the wire fencing and counted six frogs, the most yet. There were three on the bank and two in the pond with their noses sticking out of the water. Another had settled himself among the flowers.

Then Anna-Magdalena tried to stand on her head. She hadn't been making much progress lately. The second leg just wouldn't go up in the air, so she turned a somersault instead. She sat on the steps. She wished she were still at Ollie's playing with the puppy.

After a little while, her mum came out and joined her. Mum said, 'You know the chocolate Ollie wanted to give his puppy and you told him not to?'

Anna-Magdalena nodded. 'Chocolate's not good for dogs, I told him.'

Mum said, 'But you didn't give him a chance to tell you that it *wasn't* chocolate. It's a special treat that's good for puppies. It's chewy for puppy teeth and has vitamins in it to make them grow. It's not real chocolate at all.'

Anna-Magdalena's eyes grew big and her mouth made a round 'O'.

'So you see,' said Mum, 'You truly need to say "sorry" to Ollie.'

As Mum stood up to go back into the house, she said, 'Let's think of something nice to do for Ollie. You think and I'll think. Then we'll decide together.'

Anna-Magdalena walked round and round the garden thinking and thinking.

At last she ran into the house to tell her mum. She'd thought of just the right thing to please Ollie. It was something fun to do as well. Wasn't that lucky!

6

Anna-Magdalena
Ends a Fight

Anna-Magdalena had just had a brilliant idea. She and her friend Ollie had had a silly fight about his puppy and Ollie had hurt his arm. Now Anna-Magdalena had thought of just the right way to say 'sorry'.

She hurried in from the garden to find her mum and tell her the idea. It was a hot summer's afternoon, so she asked, 'Can I make ice lollies and give Ollie one?'

Mum smiled. 'A lolly for Ollie. It even rhymes. That's bound to be a good idea. It's certainly better than anything *I* thought of.'

Anna-Magdalena asked, 'Can I make special ones? With three colours? They're best.'

Mum agreed and she went to get out the things Anna-Magdalena needed. She put them all on the kitchen table. There was a plastic tray with six spaces in it for six plastic containers shaped like lollies. There were bottles of orange, lime and blackcurrant squash. Then Mum handed Anna-Magdalena two small plastic jugs. One was empty, the other had water in it.

Anna-Magdalena put on her apron and knelt on a chair. First, she fitted all the lolly-shaped containers into the spaces on the tray.

'Which flavour first?' asked Mum.

'Blackcurrant,' decided Anna-Magdalena.

Mum poured some of the blackcurrant juice into the empty jug. 'Remember to add the same amount of water,' she said. 'Up to here.' She pointed to a mark on the jug.

Carefully, Anna-Magdalena measured water into the dark red liquid. Then she poured the blackcurrant and water mixture into the bottom of the six lolly-shaped holders. She splashed some on the table by accident. Mum wiped up the puddle and then slid the tray of lollies into the freezer at the top of the fridge.

'I'll call you in half an hour,' Mum said, 'and we'll check on them.'

Anna-Magdalena went to play ball with Patch in the garden. She came back to the kitchen to see if they were ready three times before the half-hour was over. She hadn't realized that half an hour was so long.

On the third time Mum took the tray out of the freezer for inspection. The blackcurrant mixture had to be just right for Anna-Magdalena's next job. It had to be frozen hard enough to hold a lolly stick upright, but not frozen so hard that the stick wouldn't go in.

The freezing point *was* just right. Anna-Magdalena placed a stick into each starter lolly. Back into the freezer went the tray and Anna-Magdalena returned to the garden to play. She drew a house in coloured chalks on the garden path. When she had designed a family of chalk people for the house, it was time for the next lolly stage.

'Which flavour in the middle?' Mum enquired.

'Green,' Anna-Magdalena said.

The sticks were now frozen hard in the red blackcurrant bit. So Anna-Magdalena measured and poured the lime squash and water mixture into the ice lolly containers. The green liquid spread round the standing sticks.

'Leave enough space for the orange,' said Mum. Anna-Magdalena concentrated very hard. She completed her task very carefully and this time didn't spill any.

An hour passed while the lime flavour froze. Then at last Anna-Magdalena could finish her surprise for Ollie. She filled each lolly container right up to the top with a mixture of orange squash and water.

When she had done the last one, she looked up at her mum. 'D'you think Ollie will like my lollies?' What if he didn't, she worried, blowing the straight orange fringe off her forehead.

Mum said, smiling, 'I'm sure he will. Now we'll leave the lollies overnight to freeze really firm. Tomorrow, I'll let Ollie's mum know you're coming with a surprise.'

Next afternoon Anna-Magdalena set off with a little bag containing two ice lollies still in their plastic holders.

Ollie knew she was coming with a surprise and was waiting for her in his front garden.

'H'lo, Anna,' said Ollie. 'What's in your bag?'

'I made you a surprise,' she answered and took out the lollies. 'Look, ice lollies in three colours.'

She pulled the plastic container off the first lolly and gave it to Ollie. He smiled happily at it. There was a big rounded top of frozen red blackcurrant, a narrow band of green lime, and a solid bottom of orange ice.

Anna-Magdalena's lolly looked just the same and they sat down on the grass to eat them. As they started to lick their way through the red layer, Anna-Magdalena saw that Ollie still had a plaster on his arm.

'I'm sorry about your arm,' she said, pointing to the plaster.

'It doesn't hurt now,' replied Ollie. 'My mum says I'm not to push people. Then I won't get hurt.'

Anna-Magdalena nodded. She said, 'Anyway, it's wrong to do bad to somebody, even if they do bad first.' She added, 'Jesus says that.'

'Who's Jesus?' asked Ollie.

'He's God and lives in heaven,' Anna-Magdalena said, pointing up at the sky. 'He looks after us.'

'Oh,' said Ollie, 'I don't know about him.'

Anna-Magdalena's tongue made a swirl round the ice lolly to catch all the drips. 'We learn about Jesus at Sunday school. You can come if you want to.' She looked at her ice lolly. 'I'm starting green. Are you on green yet?'

He was. In fact, Ollie had almost finished his lime layer. 'This is a good lolly,' he said, admiringly.

By the time the two children had licked and dribbled their way through the orange layer, they were sticky and they were good friends again. Their fight was forgotten.

Anna-Magdalena told Ollie about the frogs in the bean pond. So they asked Ollie's mum if he could go with Anna-Magdalena to see them. When they got to Anna-Magdalena's house, her mum and baby Luke were in the garden.

'Did you like the ice lolly?' Mum asked Ollie.

He grinned. Then he spun round and round and collapsed dizzily into the grass.

'That means yes,' Anna-Magdalena told her mum, laughing. Ollie sat up and Mum opened the gate so they could see the pond properly.

Anna-Magdalena showed Ollie the flowers, fish and frogs. One frog sat on a lily pad so he was very easy to see.

There were insects who lived on the pond now too. Anna-Magdalena pointed them out. 'They're called pond skaters, my mummy says.'

The children watched fascinated as the skaters dashed around on the surface of the water. They were very fierce, charging each other and fighting for space on the pond.

'The skaters are pushing,' Anna-Magdalena said.

'There's lots of room on the pond,' Ollie said. 'Why do they have to fight each other?'

'Silly skaters,' said Anna-Magdalena.

'Silly skaters,' said Ollie, agreeing with his friend.

Anna-Magdalena
and the Crab Contest

One day in the summer holidays Uncle Andy took Anna-Magdalena to the seaside for the day. Uncle Andy always had brilliant ideas for things to do and today he said to Anna-Magdalena, 'I've got a surprise for you.'

'What is it? What is it?' she cried, excitedly.

'We're going crab fishing,' he said.

As they drove along the harbour of the little town, looking for a place to park, Uncle Andy pointed to a sign. It said:

CHILDREN'S CRAB FISHING CONTEST TODAY. ENTRY 50p. HARBOUR SHOP.

'I can catch a big crab,' said Anna-Magdalena confidently, though she had no idea how to do it.

Uncle Andy nodded in agreement. After all, Anna-Magdalena was a small but determined person.

Anna-Magdalena felt a sudden emptiness inside. She said, 'I'm hungry.'

'Me too,' said Uncle Andy.

They found a space for the car and went to the fish and chip shop nearby. The sun shone brightly. They sat on a bench facing the harbour to watch the boats and unwrapped their fish and chips. They ate hot, crisp battered fish with their fingers and shared a large portion of chips. Then they washed it all down with cans of cold, fizzy lemonade.

'Good lunch, Maggle-Waggle?' asked Uncle Andy cheerfully.

Maggle-Waggle was a new version of her name. Anna-Magdalena sighed. Whatever was to be done with Uncle Andy? He never, ever called her by her proper name. Suddenly she remembered an old book her mum had read to her.

She nodded in answer to Uncle Andy's question. 'Good lunch, Andy Pandy,' she replied with a little smile.

Uncle Andy gave a great laugh. 'I *hate* being called Andy Pandy. They used to call me that at school. You win, Anna-Magdalena.'

The small person so named grinned from ear to ear. It was the first time she could ever remember Uncle Andy saying her name just as it should be. This was going to be a great day.

When they had finished eating, they gathered up their scraps and empty drink cans and dropped them into a litter bin. Then they washed their hands at an outdoor tap and set off to register Anna-Magdalena for the crab fishing competition at the harbour shop.

'Are you a crab fisherman?' the man behind the counter asked Anna-Magdalena, smiling.

'Yes,' she replied, though she still had no idea what you had to do to catch a crab.

Uncle Andy filled in her name, address, and age on the entry form and paid the 50p.

'The money's for the lifeboat fund,' the man explained to Anna-Magdalena. 'The lifeboat crew save people who are in trouble on the sea,' he told her. Then he looked at her entry form. 'You will be in the under-eights section,' he said. 'Two prizes will be awarded in that age-group. One for the biggest crab and the other for catching the most crabs.'

More children were coming to sign up, so the man gave Anna-Magdalena her ticket. It was number 15. 'Good luck,' he said and pointed to a map on the wall behind him. 'The contest starts here at two o'clock.'

Uncle Andy studied the map. Anna-Magdalena looked, too. It was a plan of the place where the contest was being held.

It was time to gather their crab fishing equipment. Uncle Andy and Anna-Magdalena walked back to the car and took out a large bucket and a ball of string. Next, they headed for the shed on the harbour that sold fresh fish.

Anna-Magdalena was so excited she ran all the way. The shed smelled funny—all fishy and seasidy.

'Do you sell bait for the crab contest?' asked Uncle Andy.

The owner nodded and wrapped up a parcel of fish scraps and fish heads.

'That's 25p,' he said to Uncle Andy. 'Good luck,' he said to Anna-Magdalena.

'I'm going to catch the most,' she told him.

'Good for you,' the fish seller replied and gave her a thumbs up sign.

It was only half past one but they headed for the contest area. 'If we're early, we can find a good place to fish,' Uncle Andy said.

The contest was being held along the banks of a little rocky inlet and was roped off to show the fishing area. Uncle Andy and Anna Magdalena strolled along the banks, looking. Anna-Magdalena didn't know what she was looking for but she looked anyway.

Suddenly Uncle Andy said, 'Here! Put your bucket here and claim this spot.' So Anna-Magdalena did just that.

'Why's it good?' she wanted to know.

Her uncle explained that there was a flat rock to stand on, just big enough for one person to fish. There were other rocks and a picnic table nearby. 'People probably fish for crabs here,' he said. 'I expect bits of food get dropped into the water and the crabs are used to feeding round the rocks.'

Uncle Andy started to get everything ready. Anna-Magdalena unwrapped the package of fish scraps. 'Pooh,' she cried. 'They smell!'

Uncle Andy got out his penknife and cut the scraps of

fish into smaller chunks. He tied a stone onto the end of a long piece of string to weigh it down, then he helped Anna-Magdalena to tie on two chunks of fish.

It was nearly two o'clock and a number of children had arrived and found places to fish. About five metres from Anna-Magdalena another little girl stood on the bank. She and her mum were tying bits of meat on to a string.

Anna-Magdalena went to look. 'We've got fish on our string,' she said.

The girl's mum looked up. 'We brought this meat from home, but fish might be better.' She patted her daughter on the head. 'This is Lisa,' she said. 'What's your name?'

'Anna-Magdalena.'

'What a lovely name,' said Lisa's mum.

'An-na-mag-da-le-na,' Lisa said slowly, rolling her tongue correctly around the long name.

Anna-Magdalena smiled. She was pleased. She liked Lisa. Lisa smiled back.

Anna-Magdalena returned to her pitch. A loud whistle blew and the competitors scrambled to begin fishing.

Anna-Magdalena wrapped the string round her hand, as Uncle Andy had shown her, and lowered the crab-line into the water. Almost at once, she asked, 'Can I look?'

'Give the crabs a chance to find you first,' advised Uncle Andy. 'They're not riding motorbikes, you know.'

Anna-Magdalena giggled. She waited a minute. She pulled up the line. Nothing. She fished for another couple of minutes and drew in the line again. One of the fish chunks had vanished. But a little browny-green crab clung to the other chunk.

'I've got one! I've got one!' Anna-Magdalena shouted, jumping up and down and nearly knocking the crab back into the water.

Uncle Andy cried, 'Careful!' and then 'Well done!' He scooped their bucket into the water and filled it half full. Then he took the little crab off the line and showed it to Anna-Magdalena.

The crab waved its claws and looked at her. Or so she thought, because the eyes were on short stalks that moved. It had a flattish shell and four legs on each side as well as the two claws.

'That was the one with the motorbike,' said Uncle Andy, laughing. He put the crab into the bucket and they tied two new bits of fish on to the string. A few minutes later, Anna-Magdalena caught another crab. It was smaller than the first one.

'You want to take this one off, Anna-Banana?' asked Uncle Andy with a twinkle in his eye.

Anna-Magdalena looked at the little crab waving its claws at her. She shivered a little and blew the fringe off her forehead. Then she gritted her teeth and said, 'OK, Andy Pandy.'

Uncle Andy grinned. 'Hold the shell between your thumb and first finger like this,' he said. 'Then it

can't pinch your hand with its claws.'

Very carefully, Anna-Magdalena picked the crab off the chunk of fish. In a great rush she dropped it into the bucket. 'Brave girl!' Uncle Andy said.

'I've got *two*,' Anna-Magdalena called happily over to Lisa.

But Lisa shook her head. 'No luck so far,' her mum said, as she peered into the water.

Uncle Andy took some fish scraps over to Lisa and her mum. 'Maybe you'll do better with fish and we've got plenty,' he said. He tied two bits tightly onto Lisa's string.

Meanwhile, the big boy on the other side of Anna-Magdalena had caught an enormous crab. It was bound to be the winner for the older age-group.

Uncle Andy had picked a really good place to fish. Anna-Magdalena pulled in four more crabs, one after the other. They were all quite small, but now she had six crabs.

'Let's go for a big one,' suggested Uncle Andy. He tied a large fish head onto the line.

Anna-Magdalena lowered the line into the water and waited. Nothing happened for a while. Then, with a shout of delight, she pulled up a huge crab. It wasn't quite as large as the big boy's catch, but Uncle Andy said it would have a good chance to be biggest in the younger age-group.

Lisa came over to see it. She looked into the bucket at the seven crabs swimming round.

'I didn't catch *any*,' she said sadly and her big brown eyes filled with tears.

Then Anna-Magdalena's face clouded over, too. Uncle Andy knelt beside Lisa. 'It's not your fault,' he said kindly. 'But your place is sandy. The crabs don't expect to find food there.'

'Suppose . . .' his voice trailed away. He went over to Anna-Magdalena and talked to her quietly. 'Would you let Lisa fish on your rock?' he asked. 'It probably means you won't catch the most, but you have a good chance of winning a prize for the biggest crab.'

Anna-Magdalena felt mixed up inside. She wanted to count up as many crabs as she could. It would be so lovely to catch the most.

'Think how you'd feel if you hadn't caught any,' added Uncle Andy.

Anna-Magdalena decided. 'Lisa,' she said. 'Come and fish here. It's a good place.' There wasn't much time left. Lisa's mum quickly brought over the line with two big pieces of fish tied on it. Lisa dropped the string in and, just a few moments later, hauled up her first crab. It was a middle-sized crab. Lisa beamed at it proudly. Her mum took it off the bait and dropped it into Lisa's bucket.

Anna-Magdalena fished in Lisa's place but she didn't catch anything more. Just before the final whistle blew, Lisa pulled in the tiniest crab they'd ever seen. It wasn't much bigger than a small spider, Anna-Magdalena thought. Lisa put the tiny crab into her bucket herself. She was all smiles as she peered in at her two crabs.

163

'Thank you,' Lisa's mum said to Anna-Magdalena. 'That was really kind of you to let Lisa use your good fishing place.'

Lisa and Anna-Magdalena queued together at the stand to have their crabs counted and weighed. The grown-ups at the stand admired Anna-Magdalena's big crab. But it was ten grams lighter than the heaviest weighed in her age-group. Seven crabs was the most caught so far in the under-eights section, but Anna-Magdalena had looked in the bucket of a boy behind her in the queue. He had eight crabs. So now she knew she wouldn't win any prizes.

Uncle Andy knew it too. He looked down at her solemn face. 'No prizes, but we had lots of fun and that's what it's all about,' he said gently. He took her by the hand. 'And you did the right thing to share with Lisa.'

When all the weighing and counting was finished, the children put their crabs back into the water and then it was time to make the awards. In the end, it turned out that both Anna-Magdalena and Uncle Andy were wrong about the prizes.

First of all, every entrant got a lollipop whether they caught anything or not. Anna-Magdalena was pleased about that. Then the prize-giver announced, 'Every year I have a few extra prizes of my choice to give out.' He cleared his throat. 'So for the very, very smallest crab caught, would ticket number 25 please come forward.'

Lisa squealed with excitement. She was number 25.

She went up to collect a little china crab as a prize. Then the man made another announcement.

'The last prize is for the little girl who *almost* won in both categories. She had the second biggest crab *and* the second highest number caught.'

He looked around the group. 'So will ticket 15 please come to the stand.'

Number 15, a small person with orange hair and a radiant smile, rushed forward. She raced back to Uncle Andy carrying a little green china crab just like Lisa's.

It had been a great day.

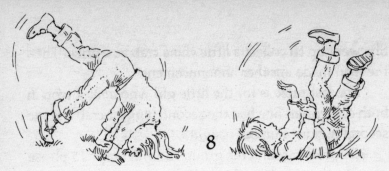

8

Anna-Magdalena
has a Trim

Anna-Magdalena was studying her little brother's head with great attention. She looked all round it and all over it and frowned. But Luke just bobbed up and down happily, saying 'Bapa,' and then, 'bapa poo dingga.'

Anna-Magdalena, still frowning, asked her mum, 'When's God going to give Luke some hair?'

'I don't know,' Mum said, looking up from sorting laundry. 'Luke's got *some* hair.'

Anna-Magdalena looked at the baby's head again. All she could see was the thinnest little covering of baby fuzz.

'It's not real hair,' she said. 'Will he be bald all his life?' she asked, blowing her thick, long, orange fringe off her forehead.

Mum laughed and said, 'No, he won't. Babies change and grow at different times and in different ways.' Then she told Anna-Magdalena how she had taken Luke to the clinic for a checkup the week before. One baby the same age had lots of hair and lots of teeth. But he couldn't pull himself up to standing like Luke.

Mum looked fondly at her son who was trying to stand at that very moment. She said, 'Each of us is a different, one-only, special person, special to God and special in the world.'

She moved a basket of folded towels and baby sheets to one side and began to sort a big pile of socks. 'There's only one Luke with almost no hair,' she said. 'And there's only one Anna-Magdalena.' She smiled at her daughter. 'So, since there's only one you, it's good to try being the best you that you can possibly be.'

Anna-Magdalena lay down on the carpet to think this over. How can I be the best me, she wondered. She thought for a while. Well, if she could *really* learn to stand on her head, for one thing. So she tried. For once both legs kicked in the air for an instant before she rolled over. That *was* better, she decided, but not 'best' yet.

Mum asked, 'Will you help me, please? Put these socks and underclothes in your drawer. You know where.'

Anna-Magdalena, wanting to be a 'best' helper, took the things. She made two trips into her bedroom with little stacks of clean laundry and put them away. 'More?' she asked, standing again ready in front of her mum.

'No, that's all. Thank you for your help,' said Mum. She looked at Anna-Magdalena and said thoughtfully, 'Speaking of hair . . .' her voice trailed away. She took her daughter by the shoulders and turned her round, looking at her carefully. 'How would you like to go to the hairdresser's for a proper haircut?'

This was a surprise. Mum always cut her hair, usually when Anna-Magdalena complained about the fringe hanging in her eyes.

Mum said encouragingly, 'A real hairdresser will shape it properly. You'll look really nice.'

That sounded all right to Anna-Magdalena. So Mum phoned and made an appointment for that very afternoon.

When they caught the bus, Anna-Magdalena recognized the number on the front of it. 'It's the swimming bus!' she said.

'That's right,' said Mum. 'We'll be catching it again when you start your new swimming club.'

'Tadpoles,' Anna-Magdalena said happily, remembering its name.

The journey to the hairdresser's was much shorter than the one to the swimming pool. So very soon, Anna-Magdalena, her mum and her little brother arrived at the shop.

'My name's Louise,' said a young woman with a great cloud of curly dark hair. 'Who's having a cut, then?' she asked, looking down at Anna-Magdalena standing beside Luke in his pushchair.

'It's me,' said Anna-Magdalena, 'not him.' She pointed at her little brother. They both gazed at Luke and giggled. He wriggled with joy and gave them a big, four-toothed smile.

'He's got teeth anyway,' Anna-Magdalena said, wanting to mention one of his good points.

Then Louise and Mum began to discuss what sort of cut Anna-Magdalena should have. 'A better shape,' said Mum, 'and shorter.'

Anna-Magdalena had a special high chair which fitted on top of the ordinary grown-up's chair. So that Mum and Luke in his pushchair could fit in, Louise turned Anna-Magdalena's chair to the side. Now the big mirror was beside Anna-Magdalena, not in front of her. This gave her a grand view of everything going on in the shop.

In front of her a woman was having squares of silver paper stuck to her head. Anna-Magdalena thought she looked like a spaceman. Another customer had a thin, tight cap fitted onto her head. The hairdresser pulled bits of hair through little holes in the cap and lathered on a purply-grey goo.

Anna-Magdalena was fascinated. 'What are they doing?' she asked Louise. 'Will I get silver paper or a hat?'

Louise answered, 'They're changing the ladies' hair colour. You don't want a new colour, do you? Yours is such a lovely, bright shade.'

Anna-Magdalena was pleased. No, she didn't want a new colour.

Snip, snip, snip went Louise's scissors. It tickled a bit when she cut round the neck. Anna-Magdalena scrunched up her shoulders.

Louise and Mum talked quietly sometimes. Anna-Magdalena, however, was so interested in what was going on in the other chairs that she didn't pay much attention to them.

A boy came in and asked for a step haircut. Anna-Magdalena saw that this meant lots of hair on top and hardly any below. A girl whose head had been covered in tiny curlers turned out to have hair that looked like wiggly lines. Anna-Magdalena tried to imagine herself with wiggly-line hair.

Louise noticed her watching the girl. 'She's had a perm,' she explained. 'Her hair was straight before and now it's curly.'

This was a surprising place, Anna-Magdalena decided. People came in and changed themselves into something else.

A few more snips. Louise brushed round Anna-Magdalena's neck with a soft brush and took the towel from around her shoulders. Then she turned the chair so that her young customer faced the mirror.

Anna-Magdalena got a terrible shock.

Staring back from the mirror was a little boy with orange hair. His eyes grew round as saucers and he looked upset. He blew on his short fringe.

'Is that me?' Anna-Magdalena asked her mum. She knew it was but she could hardly believe it. This wasn't her at her best. This was someone different.

Mum said encouragingly, 'It's a smart, short cut for summer. It'll keep you cool.'

At this moment, Anna-Magdalena thought she didn't care about being cool.

Louise said gently, 'I think it's lovely. Your head is the right shape for a short cut. But it may take you a while to get used to it.'

Anna-Magdalena didn't say anything. She glanced down at Luke and he held out his chubby arms to her. 'Poo dinga,' he said, smiling. He still knows me, she thought to herself. So that's something.

A rather quiet family returned home on the bus. When Anna-Magdalena caught sight of her reflection in the bus window, a boy stared back. It was strange to look so different. She ran her hand up the stubbly back of her head. It was strange to *feel* so different.

At home Anna-Magdalena went into Mum's and Gerald's bedroom and gazed in the full-length mirror. Mum came in behind her. She said, 'If you really don't like it, it will grow longer quite soon. You just need to wait a bit.'

That evening Gerald came home, whistling happily. 'Hi, Mags,' he called to her. She was helping her mum lay the table for tea. 'How's my girl?' he asked. He scooped her up and put her on his shoulder.

'You knew it was me?' she asked timidly, peering down at him.

'How d'you mean?' he asked, puzzled. He glanced up at her. 'Oh, the new hairdo! It's great, isn't it?'

He sat her down on a chair. 'That's for Tadpoles, I suppose. You'll swim fast as anything with no hair to drag you back.'

'Fast as anything,' Anna-Magdalena repeated slowly. She smiled for the first time since the haircut. 'Fast as anything,' she said again, thinking hard about being the best swimmer she could possibly be.

9

Anna-Magdalena
Lays a Trail

Anna-Magdalena was all dressed up in her best yellow shorts with a matching top. She was going with Neville, her friend from Sunday school, to an adventure park.

There would be thrilling rides and a picnic and a Red Indian village to visit. Anna-Magdalena was so excited that she was already standing by the front window watching for the car.

'It's too early, Mags,' said Mum. 'There's half an hour still to go.' Just as she finished speaking, the phone rang.

Anna-Magdalena didn't notice her mum's face change as she listened. She said, 'I'm so sorry. I do hope he'll be better soon.' She paused and then said, 'Don't worry. I'll tell her. Goodbye.'

Mum came over to Anna-Magdalena at the window and knelt down beside her. 'I've got bad news about your outing,' she said and put her arm around Anna-Magdalena's shoulders. 'That was Neville's mum on the phone. Neville's ill. He's got some kind of virus. I'm afraid the trip to the adventure park will have to be put off.'

Anna-Magdalena's face crumpled and her mouth began to tremble.

'Neville's mum says she's really sorry to disappoint you, but they will plan the outing for another day soon,' said Mum.

Two big tears stood in Anna-Magdalena's blue eyes. She blinked and the tears splashed out, but she didn't really cry. She just stood looking at her mum with a very sad face.

'Why don't you make a get well card for Neville?' Mum suggested. 'And while you do that, I'll see if I can arrange something else for you to do today.'

Anna-Magdalena got out her coloured pens. She slowly folded a piece of white paper twice to make a card shape. 'A flower design would be pretty for a card,' Mum said.

Anna-Magdalena set to work. A flower design wasn't what she had in mind at all. She would draw a Red Indian to remind Neville that they were still going to the adventure park. She got out her book about cowboys and Indians and looked at it. Then she drew a man with red, yellow and green stripes to make an Indian feather headdress standing up from his head.

Anna-Magdalena drew the outline and coloured it in very carefully. When she had nearly finished, she said to her mum, 'We can pray for Neville tonight and ask God to make him better. Then we can go tomorrow.'

'Not tomorrow, Mags,' Mum said. 'Tomorrow's

Sunday and there's church and Sunday school in the morning. Anyway, the adventure park trip needs a whole day.' She got out an envelope for Neville's card and laid it on the table. 'But I'm glad you thought of praying for Neville,' she added. 'We'll ask God to make him better and to comfort him while he's ill.'

Anna-Magdalena made some red, yellow and green stripes across the back of the card and handed it to her mum to write a message. Mum wrote inside the card,

Get well soon, Neville. We're sorry you're ill. Love from

Then Anna-Magdalena wrote her name. She thought it looked very good, hardly wobbly at all.They posted the card in the postbox on the corner and then Mum told Anna-Magdalena her new plan for the afternoon.

Just after lunch, Uncle Henry and Aunty Cath, who was Mum's sister, came to pick up Anna-Magdalena in the car. They were going for a walk in the woods. And Uncle Henry had promised Anna-Magdalena a surprise.

It was a sunny day and there were lots of cars in the car park near the entrance to the woods. In the corner was an ice-cream van, too. Anna-Magdalena looked hopefully toward the van, but Uncle Henry was already striding off in the opposite direction with a rucksack on his back. Aunty Cath and Anna-Magdalena hurried after him.

At the start of a winding path, Uncle Henry stopped and took something out of his rucksack. It was a thin, red cardboard circle, a bit like a crown, and it had blue-grey pigeon feathers sellotaped to it.

'I'm going to lay an Indian trail for you and Aunty Cath to follow,' Uncle Henry explained. 'Here is your Indian headdress. You'll need it if you want to find my signs.'

Anna-Magdalena clapped her hands in delight and jammed the feather headdress on her head. She'd played cowboys and Indians with Ollie and she knew what to do. She danced round slapping the palm of her hand against her mouth and shouting, 'Whoo, wah, wah, wah! Whoo, wah, wah, wah!'

Uncle Henry said with a big grin, 'I think you have the idea.'

Aunty Cath and Anna-Magdalena waited behind a tree so they couldn't see which way Uncle Henry was marking out his trail. After about five minutes they heard a high-pitched whistle. That was the signal to start following the trail.

Anna-Magdalena found the first trail mark. In the middle of the path was an arrow made from little stones. It pointed straight ahead, so the two pathfinders kept walking.

Next they came to a place where the path divided. Anna-Magdalena saw an arrow made from small sticks. It pointed towards the path going off to the left, so they followed it.

Aunty Cath discovered the next pointer. It was an arrow chalked on a tree. It pointed to the right, away from the path.

Now the trail was harder to follow. They had to look carefully for all the signs: chalk marks on a big rock; pointers made from leaves; and more stick and stone arrows. After a while, they came to an open space where a family had just spread out a blanket for a picnic. They watched Aunty Cath and Anna-Magdalena walk round and round, looking for a sign.

'We're following an Indian trail,' Aunty Cath explained, though she suspected they might have guessed that from Anna-Magdalena's headdress.

The grown-ups nodded politely, and the two children just stared, with their mouths open.

'They're prob'ly sitting on our arrow,' Anna-Magdalena whispered to her aunt. She was just about to ask them if she could look under their blanket when they both saw the next sign.

A clump of tall grass was bent over and pointing away from the clearing. Could *that* be it? Sure enough, just a few metres away was an arrow of small pebbles which directed them down a narrow downhill path.

The path led in to another sunny, grassy open space where they found Uncle Henry. He was unpacking his rucksack.

'So soon?' he enquired when he saw them. 'I laid a really difficult trail. I thought you wouldn't be here for hours and I could drink all the tea and eat all the bickies myself.'

'We're too fast for you!' cried Anna-Magdalena, and she did another Red Indian dance. 'Whoo, wah, wah,

wah!' shouted Anna-Magdalena.

Suddenly she realized she was hungry, so she sat down. Aunty Cath and Uncle Henry drank some tea from a flask and there was a can of fizzy lemonade for Anna-Magdalena. And chocolate biscuits. Anna-Magdalena ate four of them. They were only small so she had to have lots, she said, and Uncle Henry agreed.

While Aunty Cath and Uncle Henry relaxed in the sunshine, Anna-Magdalena tried standing on her head. Her uncle watched as she kicked up her legs and tumbled this way and that.

After a while he stood up and took her by the hand. 'Come with me, Sausage,' he said, and they walked together to the nearest tree at the edge of the clearing.

Anna-Magdalena put her head down on the ground in the soft leaves, as Uncle Henry instructed. Then he lifted up her legs and rested them against the trunk of the tree. So there she was, standing on her head against the tree all by herself and wearing a big smile.

'It's even easier up against a flat wall at home,' Uncle Henry told her. Anna-Magdalena rolled down from the tree, still beaming, and said she would try it.

Aunty Cath picked the leaves out of Anna-Magdalena's hair. 'Lucky it's so short, otherwise we'd be here all day,' she said. When it was more or less clean again, Anna-Magdalena whispered in Aunty Cath's ear, and they both looked enquiringly at Uncle Henry.

Aunty Cath said, 'Our chief scout wants to lay a trail for you to find. Are you game?'

He was, of course. Anna-Magdalena and Aunty Cath set off to lay the hardest trail they possibly could. They put down arrows made of tiny pebbles and sycamore seeds and long stems of grass. They made their trail twist and turn. Several groups of people walking their dogs stopped to watch them.

As Anna-Magdalena was constructing an arrow of small twigs, she suddenly heard a little tinkling tune, not very far away. She changed the direction of her arrow and pointed it towards the sound. Aunty Cath understood at once and laughed.

From there, Anna-Magdalena put down the arrows in a straight, easy line. Uncle Henry very soon found out that the straight easy line led directly to the ice-cream van in the car park. Beside the van waited two trail-blazers.

They were waiting for someone to buy them very large ice-creams. And they weren't disappointed.

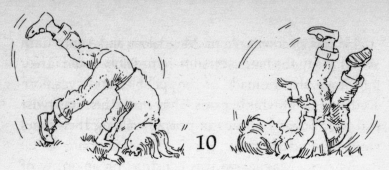

10

Anna-Magdalena
and the Green Team

One day Anna-Magdalena asked Ollie if he'd like to go to Sunday school with her next Sunday. It was a good day to go because later on there was going to be a picnic with sports and games.

So, on Sunday morning, Anna-Magdalena, her mum, and her stepdad Gerald, took Ollie with them to church. First, Ollie met Mrs Lander, the Sunday school teacher. 'She tells good stories,' Anna-Magdalena told Ollie. Then he met the other children in the class—Jack, Polly, Rajinder, Tommy and Kevin.

Anna-Magdalena looked round for Neville, her special friend. He wasn't there. Was he still ill, she wondered? He'd been too poorly to go on the adventure park outing they'd planned. But a few moments later, someone pushed open the door and a face peeped round. It was Neville!

'Oh, Neville, we missed you last Sunday,' said Mrs Lander. 'Are you feeling all right now?' Neville smiled and nodded a big nod. He never said very much. Which was just as well, as Anna-Magdalena made up for it in Sunday school.

The children settled down on the rug to hear the story. Ollie sat on one side of Anna-Magdalena and Neville sat on the other. Mrs Lander was going to tell them a story about Jesus.

Jesus lived on earth a long time ago. People kept coming to find him. Some of them were ill and Jesus made them feel better. And lots of people brought their little children and babies for Jesus to bless. Some of Jesus' friends scolded the mums and dads. They said Jesus shouldn't be wasting his time with children and babies.

But Jesus told his friends they were wrong. He told them that children were the most important of all. He said, 'You grown-ups must become like little children to go into God's kingdom.' Then he took the children into his arms and asked God to bless them.

Anna-Magdalena had heard this story before. Mum and Gerald often read her Bible stories at bedtime. This story always made her feel special. 'Each one of you is as important to Jesus as those children who lived long ago,' said Mrs Lander, looking round at the children sitting on the rug.

Anna-Magdalena, feeling important, smiled. Neville, who was shy and usually didn't feel very important, beamed. Ollie looked thoughtful.

After the story, all the children moved to the work-table. 'We usually make something to help us remember the story,' Mrs Lander told Ollie. 'But today is different. We're going to make a surprise for the picnic.'

'What is it?' asked Anna-Magdalena at once. She liked surprises.

Mrs Lander smiled and said, 'It won't be a surprise if I tell you, will it?'

She handed each child three small cardboard circles. Each circle had a small safety pin taped to the back of it. Mrs Lander put some paintbrushes in the centre of the table and some tiny pots of gold paint.

'Paint gold on the plain side of each circle,' Mrs Lander told them. 'It's easiest if you hold it by the safety pin while you paint.'

Anna-Magdalena held her disc by its safety pin, and painted the plain side very carefully.

When the children had finished painting their circles, they put them on a big tray to dry. Then Mrs Lander divided the class into groups of two or three. She gave each group a small cardboard tray to paint gold. She also put out some new brushes and some blue paint.

'But what's it for?' asked Anna-Magdalena.

'You'll see,' said Mrs Lander, smiling.

Ollie, Neville, and Anna-Magdalena painted a tray together. While Ollie and Anna-Magdalena slapped paint on the centre of the tray, Neville painted careful designs round the edge. 'Neville is the best at painting,' Anna-Magdalena told Ollie. Neville didn't say anything, but he looked pleased. His ears went pink, too.

Every time Anna-Magdalena tried to ask Mrs Lander

184

what the circles and trays were for, Mrs Lander just smiled and said, 'You'll see.'

When the trays were painted, the children washed their hands and the class finished with a prayer.

Now it was time for the picnic. It was going to be in the park near the church.

Anna-Magdalena and Ollie helped Mum and Gerald spread a rug on the ground and watched with interest as every family who came put their different kinds of food out on a large picnic table.

There was cold chicken, potato salad, tomato and lettuce salad, cheese pie, curried vegetables and rice, spicy meatballs, cheese and pineapple on sticks, sandwiches, crisps, buttered rolls, and lots of cold drinks.

Before they began, they said a prayer to thank God for the good food. Then they all tucked in. The grown-ups were so busy talking that the children ate whatever they wanted. Kevin just ate crisps, his favourite food. Anna-Magdalena picked the tomatoes out from the salad, leaving all the lettuce. Neville ate cheese and pineapple. Ollie ate meatballs with his fingers.

Then *everybody* ate strawberries. Everybody liked strawberries. Everybody, except baby Luke. Anna-Magdalena had saved him her biggest strawberry, but when he put it in his mouth, he pulled a face and spat it straight out! Mum and Gerald laughed, but Anna-Magdalena felt a bit cross. He'd *wasted* her biggest strawberry.

She wasn't cross for long though because it was time for the games. All the grown-ups, even grannies and granddads, and all the children were divided into teams—Red, Blue and Green. There was a prize for the best team.

Neville, Ollie and Anna-Magdalena were all in the Green team. Anna-Magdalena just couldn't wait to win the prize.

'Come on,' she said, 'We're going to win,' and she pulled Neville and Ollie off to try the egg-and-spoon race.

The egg-and-spoon race wasn't at all easy. Nobody in the Green team could balance an egg on a spoon for more than a few seconds at a time. Anna-Magdalena tried to run fast and dropped her egg again and again. Every time she had to go back to the starting line, she blew the fringe off her forehead. The last time she stepped on her egg by accident. Luckily, it was hard-boiled. The Greens came last.

'Never mind, Greens,' said the leader, who was called Danny. 'We'll do better next time.'

The next game was a silly version of musical chairs, played with picnic benches. It didn't work very well but everyone laughed a lot. The Greens came last again.

'It's our turn to win next,' Anna-Magdalena told Danny.

'Absolutely,' he said. 'Did you hear that everyone?' he called. 'Titch here says it's our turn to win!'

So Anna-Magdalena, Ollie and Neville were very keen to do their best in the obstacle race. There was a practice run to show everybody what to do and then the whistle blew.

When it was her turn, the small, determined figure of Anna-Magdalena ran forward. She had to pick up three tennis balls and throw them into a bucket. Thud went the first tennis ball. Thud went the second. After three tries, thud went the third. The Green team cheered and Anna-Magdalena raced ahead to the next obstacle.

She had to jump in and out of three cardboard boxes. Grown-ups with long legs could hop in and out easily, but Anna-Magdalena had to clamber in and out like a monkey. A very quick monkey. All her team were cheering.

Next Anna-Magdalena crawled on her tummy under some netting. After that she had to throw rings over a stick stuck in the ground. She stood as near as she could and the rings went over—one, two, three.

By now, the Green team was leading. Anna-Magdalena ran on to the last obstacle—a chair with a balloon taped to it. All she had to do was sit on it and pop it.

But Anna-Magdalena was so light, she just bobbed up and down. The balloon squidged this way and that, but it didn't break. Finally, she put her feet on the chair and gave a mighty leap up. Down she came with a B A N G !

'Go, go, go!' shouted the Greens as she tore back across the grass to touch the hand of the next player. The next three players were fast—the Greens had won!

Next came the three-legged race. The Green captain paired Anna-Magdalena with a tiny little girl called Susie who was only three. Her dad said she was too young and would fall over. But Danny urged, 'Let her try. She can go slow. It's all in fun.' He turned to Anna-Magdalena. 'Titch,

187

will you help Susie and be her partner?'

Anna-Magdalena was surprised and pleased to find she was old enough to be a helper. With a scarf, Danny tied Susie's right leg to Anna-Magdalena's left one. Off they hobbled, not fast but doing well. As Danny had suggested, Anna-Magdalena counted one-two, one-two. Their single leg went forward on 'one' and their tied together double leg went forward on 'two'.

'Well done,' cried Danny when they got to the finishing line. Susie's face was all smiles and so was Anna-Magdalena's. The Greens did well and clocked up the second quickest time overall.

The last game was rounders which the Greens won in a play-off against the Blues. The games organizer looked at his list and said, 'The Green team wins overall. Congratulations.'

All the Greens cheered, all the Reds and Blues hissed and booed and everybody laughed. When the commotion had died down, the organizer said, 'And now here's something for the winners.'

Anna-Magdalena, Ollie and Neville jumped up from where they were sitting on the grass to see what it was.

'It's our circles!' cried Anna-Magdalena.

Sure enough, the discs they had painted gold that morning now had neat black lettering which said 'Champion.' Anna-Magdalena, Neville and Ollie beamed from ear to ear as their badges were pinned on.

Then bags of sweets were passed round on three painted trays—the trays they'd painted in Sunday school.

Every child on every team received a bag of sweets.

'No sweets for the grown-ups, I'm afraid,' said the organizer. 'You'll have to make do with tea and cakes.'

After tea, the mums and dads started packing, getting ready to go home. Anna-Magdalena and her friends were showing off their best skills. Rajinder could do a cartwheel. Kevin made his eyes disappear up under his eyelids (the other children all went *ugggh*!). Neville made his ears wiggle, and Ollie showed them how he could burp whenever he wanted to (his older brother had taught him).

Anna-Magdalena suddenly said, 'I can stand on my head. Only I need a wall.'

'Why d'you need a wall?' asked Jack, who had just joined them.

'It helps,' said Anna-Magdalena, looking at the nearest tree, which had bumpy roots all round the bottom. That was no good, nowhere to put her head.

So Anna-Magdalena put her head down on the grass. From upside-down, she said, 'And then you put your legs up on the wall.' She lifted her right leg to show how it would be if there was a wall there.

She had stood on her head against the wall at home a great many times, since Uncle Henry had helped her on the trail-finding day. Now the other leg just went up, almost by itself. And there she was, balanced perfectly, upside-down, on her head and not leaning against anything!

Polly tickled her and she fell over. But Anna-Magdalena came up smiling. Now she knew she could always do it.

The Green team had won. Anna-Magdalena had a beautiful champion badge and half a bag of sweets left. She'd made friends with little Susie and had a great time with Ollie and Neville. Best of all, she'd stood on her head all by herself at last. Anna-Magdalena knew that she was the happiest girl in the whole world.

Also from Lion publishing

THE DRAGONS OF KILVE

Beth Webb

The unexpected arrival of the baby dragons—Horace, Maurice, Clarys, Sparky and Treasure—turns the peaceful life of the dragons of Kilve upside down. It leads to all sorts of adventures and mishaps: Igneous and Furnace get into a hot spot, Maurice's pride leads to a muddy fall, and Treasure lives up to her name.

The wise old Dragon Master is always close at hand to comfort, cheer and encourage the sometimes wayward dragons. And, best of all, he helps them to discover three great secrets.

ISBN 0 7459 2747 5

All Lion paperbacks are available from your local bookshop, or can be ordered direct from Lion Publishing. For a free catalogue, showing the complete list of titles available, please contact:

Customer Services Department
Lion Publishing plc
Peter's Way
Sandy Lane West
Oxford OX4 5HG

Tel: (01865) 747550
Fax: (01865) 715152